BRETT

BROTHERHOOD PROTECTORS WORLD

REGAN BLACK

Twisted Page Press LLC

BROTHERHOOD PROTECTORS

ORIGINAL SERIES BY ELLE JAMES

With special thanks to Elle James for inviting me into her world of Brotherhood Protectors.

GUARDIAN AGENCY: BRETT

ABOUT *GUARDIAN AGENCY: BRETT*

When hope is lost, truth is blurred, and your life is on the line,
it's time to call in the Guardian Agency...

She's been betrayed too often... Can a sexy new body-guard flip the script?

Nikki Weston is spending Christmas -and her birthday- in South Carolina, far from Hollywood and the prying gaze of a relentless stalker. With good friends close and a private beach outside her window, her working holiday is paradise until the stalker strikes again. Now, to protect others she must ask for help, but trust is not her strong suit.

Former Navy SEAL, Brett Robinson, is learning how to be home again after his military career ended early. Thanks to the Guardian Agency, he has found a new way to serve and a new calling as a bodyguard. When the order comes through to protect Nikki, a beautiful silver screen celebrity from a real-world threat, he figures Christmas has come early.

Unfortunately, Nikki isn't keen on a hovering bodyguard, no matter how necessary. But when the stalker escalates, Brett's best move is to fake a holiday romance worthy of the big screen. And now it really is mission impossible: save the girl without losing his heart.

Visit ReganBlack.com for a full list of books, excerpts and upcoming release dates.
For early access to new releases, exclusive prizes, and much more,
subscribe to Regan's monthly newsletter.

CHAPTER 1

HANK PATTERSON AND HIS WIFE, Sadie, walked at the edge of the surf, laughing every time their daughter, Emma, giggled as the Atlantic Ocean came up and tickled her toes. Emma loved the beach and he loved his girls. Born and raised in Montana, his career as a Navy SEAL had taken him all over the world. Now that he was done with the military, he'd built up the Brotherhood Protectors, a security service based in his hometown of Eagle Rock that primarily employed former military personnel like himself.

"Well, it isn't a white Christmas," Sadie said, "but it will be a bright one, don't you think?"

"Looks that way."

"You're sure you don't mind being away from the ranch this time of year?"

"It's Christmas every day when I'm with my girls," he replied, earning a fast kiss. "What locations do you need to visit today?" Hank asked. They were in Charleston, South Carolina so she could do some preliminary research for a new movie. She hadn't decided to take the leading role yet, but he knew she was leaning that way.

"I have a morning meeting downtown at the market," she replied. "Should be free by noon."

Between them, Emma bent over, studying a seashell stuck in the sand. At three years old she was curious about everything and Hank got a kick out of seeing the world in new ways through her innocent eyes. "Would you like us to meet you for lunch?"

"I was actually thinking about meeting Nikki at the theater," she said.

Nikki Weston was one of Sadie's best friends from the Hollywood scene. She was the guest producer for the annual production of The Nutcracker, an endeavor that raised funds for the historic Dock Street Theater as well as local theatrical groups. She was one more reason they'd made the trip, booking rooms at the same exclusive resort on the Isle of Palms.

Sadie tucked a wayward strand of hair behind her ear and stared out over the water. "You know how she took the job so she could relax and enjoy herself, but I think something is wrong."

"With the production?"

"No." Sadie shook her head. "Something else. I'm

worried about her, Hank. She's started looking for alternatives."

"What kind of alternatives?" The worry in her voice had his professional protective instincts perking up.

Sadie crouched down beside Emma, determined to uncover the rest of the newest seashell she'd found. "She wants out of Hollywood. For good this time."

Hank had heard, through Sadie, how Nikki had been raked over the coals in the tabloids and in the industry by a man who insisted she reneged on her promises. He'd managed to convince the press and several influential professionals that Nikki was flighty and unreliable, using the luck of her birth to blackball her competitors and lavish benefits on her favorite people.

It was complete fiction, but he wouldn't let up. Sadie was convinced he was behind every bit of misfortune and bad press that targeted Nikki, but so far no one could find any evidence. Nikki had retreated from the public eye, as much as that was possible for a woman of her pedigree and beauty.

"I think that jerk tormenting her has done something new, but she won't give me any details," Sadie continued. "I'm aware that a woman with her net worth must always be a little on guard." She stood, her nose wrinkling with frustration. "But come on.

I'm her best friend, you're the best in private security. She should let us help."

"Want me to talk with her? Hank offered. "I could bring someone down to keep an eye on her." He wasn't willing to relinquish the family time and make this a full-blown working weekend for both of them.

"Maybe you should." Sadie brushed sand from her hands and guided Emma back toward the resort. "If she'll listen. Most likely having a stranger hover will only put her on edge. She doesn't trust anyone after those pictures of her bedroom and the pool were leaked."

That had been rough and somehow, Nikki was blamed for pulling a publicity stunt, though Hank knew the woman was too private to take that chance.

"She's determined a change of scenery is enough, Sadie continued. "I agreed with her at first. Now I'm not sure it's enough. I'll try to get the full story at lunch."

"All right," Hank said. "Emma and I could join." He brushed a hand over his daughter's head. "She could be a distraction when I start asking questions."

"Not a bad idea," Sadie said as they crossed the boardwalk over the dunes for breakfast at the resort's outdoor dining area.

Sadie ate quickly and went upstairs to change. When she returned, wearing an emerald dress that hugged her curves and boots he knew she could run a marathon in, his heart sped up. He was the luckiest man in the world. "What's the call on lunch?"

She kissed Emma's head. "Drop in. I'll text you the address."

"Can't wait." But first he had to get his daughter cleaned up and make a couple of calls. Just in case he could convince Nikki to accept some help.

With Emma clean and in a sweet mood, Hank went in search of the head of security for the exclusive resort. It wasn't the type of meeting his daughter usually attended, but better to start teaching her the business at a young age.

Bruce Ellington met him at the front desk. He had a few years on Hank based on the graying temples and crow's feet bracketing his eyes, but he radiated fitness and confidence.

"Quite a beauty you have there," he said, smiling warmly at Emma as Hank made introductions. "Are you enjoying your stay?"

"We are," Hank said. "Beautiful place. My wife and her friends have been here before, but this is my first trip out."

"We're happy to have you," Bruce said, leading them back to his office. "What brings you to see me?"

"Nikki Weston is a good friend of ours," Hank said. "My wife is concerned that she's ignoring some trouble. I wanted to ask if you could bump up security without appearing to bump up security."

"What kind of trouble?" Bruce queried.

"She was being harassed out in California. It was basically a smear campaign by a disgruntled competitor." Hank sat down, Emma in his lap. "No physical violence, just pesky stalker-ish stuff. Sadie thinks he's done something new, but Nikki isn't talking and she's always been reluctant to trust anyone."

Bruce nodded and Hank had the distinct impression he'd seen the tabloids on Nikki and put measures in place to prevent such an embarrassing moment here.

"I don't want to overstep." Hank continued. "Nikki is very independent and self-sufficient. So far she won't even let me assign her any security support." He handed over his business card.

"That makes it more challenging," Bruce said sympathetically. "Are you worried things could turn violent?"

"There's no indication of that. I'm just hoping to keep more eyes on her."

"We can do that. Do you have a description of the man giving her grief in California?"

"Gus Haynes," Hank replied. "A quick internet search gave me way too much information on the whole mess." He waited while Bruce skimmed the first page of results.

"You really want her to have a bodyguard and she's opposed."

"Yes," Hank confirmed. Emma reached for the

shiny nameplate on Bruce's desk and Hank pulled her back.

"Oh, let her play," Bruce said, reaching into a drawer. "She can't hurt that."

Emma chattered, delighted by her prize.

"Do you have any rooms available?" Hank asked. "I've called a friend for another possible solution, assuming Nikki agrees."

"I'll make sure we have something," Bruce promised. "You might try this group too." He handed over a plain white business card with glossy black lettering.

Hank smiled at the Guardian Agency card. He'd worked a few cases with them recently and he'd sent a text message to Claudia, a member of their technical support staff, before coming to Bruce. "They have someone local?" he asked.

"Yes," Bruce said. "Please keep me in the loop. If there's anything more we can do, you can count on us."

"Thanks," Hank stood and Emma returned the nameplate before they all shook hands.

His cell phone rang as Hank and Emma returned to their room. It was Claudia.

"Hi, Hank. How are things?"

"Great. We're soaking up some warm weather and sunshine in Charleston while Sadie squeezes in some research."

"Smart time to visit," she said. "I heard Montana just got another few feet of snow."

"Something to look forward to," Hank deadpanned. "You've probably figured out I didn't call just call to say happy holidays."

Claudia chuckled. "What's up?"

"I need a discreet favor," he said. "Do you have anyone available in this area?"

"I'm sure we do." He could hear her fingers on a computer keyboard. "Is there a reason you didn't call one of your own men"

Hank gave her a rundown of Nikki's possible situation and definite resistance to accepting help.

"Interesting," Claudia said. "I've seen a couple of Haynes's movies. I like Nikki's work better."

As he'd assumed, she was reading through the information available online. Thankfully, Claudia was smart enough to read between the headlines and get the whole story. "You sure you want me to send someone in before you convince her? I would hate for my local guy to scare her."

"I'm sure. If the hotel is on alert and you have someone nearby who won't interfere, we can prevent any trouble before it starts."

"Understood." She was typing again. "I'll send you the contact information and you can forward it to Nikki. Does that work?"

"Thanks, Claudia. I owe you one."

CHAPTER 2

AT THE THEATER in downtown Charleston, Nikki kept tabs on the rehearsal, though her attention was divided. She knew Haynes was close. She couldn't see him, but she knew. Having spent much of her life on stage or in front of film crews, she understood what it felt like to be watched. What it felt like to be admired. This was different, like splinters under her skin. He was close. She had to find a way to head him off before he caused big trouble for this special production.

She rubbed her temples. Life had felt like nothing but trouble for too long. She'd done everything possible to dodge sticky issues, to avoid drama. To rise above the harassment and be the bigger person. But Gus Haynes was tenacious. He relentlessly insisted she owed him time and money. He told anyone who would listen that she'd made him promises. And too many people were willing to believe his lies. He had an uncanny ability to work public opinion, turning her preference for privacy against her.

As if her desire for peace and quiet was a tacit admission of guilt.

She didn't give interviews or answer questions about Haynes. Wouldn't fuel his obsession. With every encounter it became clear to her that the man wanted more than her influence, time, or money. He wanted to *own* her.

When invited by the local theater company to be the guest producer and director of the annual fundraising performance of The Nutcracker, she'd jumped at the chance. She'd been thrilled at the idea of spending the holidays in South Carolina, far from the constant glare of California. Delighted by the prospect of celebrating her birthday on a private beach. She'd come to work, but also to escape and get some breathing room.

It had never occurred to her that he would follow.

Back in California, her parents urged her to hire a security team, offered to send in someone from the company they kept on retainer.

She'd turned them down, having been burned one time too many by people that should've been trustworthy. She was here with friends and taking care to only be alone in her hotel room. Yes, Haynes's persistence was frightening, but she was doing her best to reject it, refusing to be a prisoner of fear.

Christmas was a week away, damn it. Along with her birthday on the twenty-fifth. She would not turn thirty shaking like a cornered rabbit. She had to find a way to put an end to this. Maybe if Haynes got too close, the local police would listen. Maybe. The authorities in California kept telling her he hadn't done anything criminal and they had no reason to bring him in.

At the sound of a happy giggle, Nikki turned. Her friend Sadie had arrived, her husband and daughter in tow. The three of them warmed her heart, Emma between her parents, each of them holding one of her hands as she scampered to keep up with them. So many tiny steps to make up for a single stride of her father and mother.

The little girl was absolutely adorable. Her eyes went wide at the sight of the pretty costumes and people bustling about, on a break before the afternoon rehearsal. She'd had to cancel lunch, but there was just enough time to give the family a full tour before things got started again.

"I wish she was old enough for me to put her on stage," Nikki said, scooping Emma into her arms. "You'd be the perfect sugar plum."

Hank barked with laughter. "Perfect is overstating it," he said with affection. "At least this season."

The entire company, from lead to the lighting

assistant cooed over Emma and tried not to gush over Sadie. The little girl brightened the day with her angelic smiles, awed eyes, and enthusiastic giggles.

While they were distracted, she pulled Hank aside. "I could use a favor," she began. "Did you happen to bring any of your bodyguards with you?"

He gave her a strange look. "No. I can rectify that with a phone call. What's going on?"

She took a deep breath. "This is the part where I sound crazy," she admitted. "I know Sadie has told you a few things about the problem child in California." Hank nodded. "And I don't have any solid proof about Haynes being the problem child. But I think he followed me here. No." She straightened her shoulders. "I *know* he did, but again, no proof."

Hank's eyebrows arched. "Here? Right now?"

"I'm sure of it," she replied. "Don't bother looking. He could be hiding anywhere in this old theater. I haven't actually seen him yet. I just know." At Hank's troubled expression, she added, "Trust me, it would be a relief to blame it on paranoia, but…"

"I believe you."

The tension gripping her shoulders broke as relief and hope flooded her system. Moments like this made it so easy to understand why Sadie was head over heels in love with her husband.

"This was on my rental car this morning." Nikki handed him the postcard advertising the production. Her name had been scratched out with some sharp object and the ballerina's white skirt had been marred by a red marker.

"You're not paranoid," Hank stated. "Someone has been close enough to figure out your rental car."

She shivered, remembering the moment that fact had dawned on her.

"I'm on it," he said. "I'll stay with you through the afternoon and get things in motion while you're working. Can you handle that?"

She was ashamed at how much she wanted to lean on him. His confidence chased away the chill of being watched. "Hank, I can't intrude on your vacation that way."

"This was a working vacation for all of us and you know it," he said.

"It wasn't supposed to be *your* working vacation," she protested. "I've held my own up to now with Haynes. I can manage another day. I feel better just asking for help."

She trusted Hank implicitly and although she didn't know who he would bring in, if they were one of his, she could deal with being shadowed. Anything to protect the production.

"Maybe, but Sadie would kill me if you're wrong." He glanced across the stage to see his wife taking pictures while one of the dancers twirled with Emma. "I'll fill her in and let you do your thing."

"Okay." Smiling, she changed the subject as Sadie and Emma joined them. "How was your fishing trip?"

"He caught our dinner," Sadie gushed. "Red snapper. The hotel is taking care of everything and will prepare it for us tonight. You have to join us. The chef assured us there will be plenty."

Nikki's heart felt lighter already. "That's the best invitation I've had all day." She kissed Emma's cheek. "I can't wait," she waved at the toddler as she darted away.

With the rehearsal underway and Hank nearby, she was able to push thoughts of Haynes to the back of her mind and focus on something positive for a change.

Brett Robinson was chopping an onion, prepping a fresh salsa for the taco dinner he had in mind. Moving the knife rapidly across the cutting board was the closest thing he'd had to danger in weeks.

His phone vibrated on the counter and a single word filled the screen: Protect

Finally. He set the knife aside and went to the sink to wash his hands. By the time his hands were dry again, the alert for an email with an attachment had joined the text message.

Both the text and the email were from Claudia, instead of his usual tech support, Tyler. Although it was rare for him to work with her, she had excellent skills and a high tolerance for sarcasm.

He couldn't wait to get moving, impatient because the Guardian Agency hadn't tapped him for a case in over a week. He was afraid he'd have the holidays off. Facing Christmas alone wasn't his idea of a good time. He needed the distractions and his career as a bodyguard provided plenty. Most of the time.

To his surprise, he discovered a certain pride in being a bodyguard. The variety of clientele and the various challenges suited him perfectly. He'd been trained by the Navy to resolve any kind of problem and he was grateful the agency picked him up when the Navy had sent him packing.

According to the message, this was a last-minute gig and he was needed in Charleston immediately, if not sooner. He chuckled. So far, so typical. Fortunately, he was less than an hour away, his go-bag always packed and ready.

He did a double-take when he saw the client's name and picture. Nikki Weston. Hell, he didn't even need the name, he was one of her top fans. He'd memorized that face years ago. Big, blue eyes balanced her sharp features and wide smile. Her hair was a mass of silky champagne-blonde waves that tumbled past her shoulders. Although the gorgeous actress hadn't appeared on-screen in recent years, she had been producing and directing several highly acclaimed movies.

Oh, this was going to be tricky, keeping his cool around a woman he'd never forgotten. He'd met her when she was part of a USO tour during his last deployment overseas. For a fleeting moment he wondered if she'd remember. Not a chance. She met thousands of people for a few seconds at a time on those trips.

She'd been so gracious. So fresh and clean and colorful. A beautiful break in the mosaic of camouflage and grit and shipping-container housing.

Yanking his mind back to the task, he opened the file and read it through once to get the gist of the situation. Possible stalker, client less than eager for protection. Great. But she was the guest director for the annual holiday fundraising production of The Nutcracker at the Dock Street Theater.

Cool. His grandmother had taken him several times when he was a kid and he knew the story inside and out.

Within 15 minutes he had his kitchen clean and his house set for an extended absence. Tossing the go-bag on the floor behind the driver's seat, he headed to Charleston. Once he reached the interstate, he used his voice-control to call Claudia.

"Merry Christmas, Brett," she answered.

"To you too." *Christmas. Nikki Weston's birthday.* He had to get a grip and he'd better start now. "So my client is working in Charleston and staying out at the Isle of Palms?"

"That's right," Claudia replied. "At the Ellington resort. We have a room for you too."

"Wow."

Guess he could cross "luxury hotel stay" off his bucket list. Too bad his grandmother wasn't alive to see this. She would've flipped. He should've thought about wardrobe expectations before he got in the car. Well, if he needed a suit, he could find one downtown. When Gamble and Swann had recruited him they'd given him a choice of regions to call home base. Nothing ever felt like home the way South Carolina did and he was glad to work primarily in familiar surroundings these days.

"What happened to Tyler?" he asked, "Not that I don't love the sound of your voice in my ear."

His normal tech assistant struck him as a young man in twenties. He had no way of knowing for sure since Guardian Agency policy was to insulate people for their own protection and overall security of the company. It had struck him as very cloak-and-dagger at first, yet there was something comforting in that need-to-know approach.

"Tyler must be using some vacation time."

"He doesn't do that often enough," Brett said. "Does Nikki know who is reporting?"

"She should know soon," Claudia said. "She didn't make the request directly. You'll coordinate with Hank Patterson and Bruce Ellington when you reach the resort. They'll fill you in on the specifics."

"How do those two tie in?"

"Right. I've got a sugar rush going. Nathan made

almond roca." She cleared her throat. "Bruce is head of resort security. Patterson is the husband of Sadie McClain, Nikki's closest friend. There is no threat to the Patterson's, and believe me, Hank can take care of himself."

"Interesting."

Claudia sighed. "Like you, he's a former Navy SEAL and runs his own security and protection service out of Montana."

"But he called us?"

"Of course. We're the best." He heard the smile in her voice.

"We're closer," he guessed at the real reason. "Plus I know the area."

"I would've thought resort security would be enough to ease Hank's concerns, but I think calling us has more to do with the client's desire for privacy and discretion than any issues with the competency of the security office."

"Must be it," Brett said. "Ellington is top of the line, whatever they touch."

"Good to know," Claudia said.

"I'll call you back when I've made contact with the client," Brett promised.

"That works. Anything you need, give a shout." She was typing on her keyboard, fingers flying by the sound of it. "I'm going to keep working background."

That would keep her busy. "She's had a few stalkers along the way," Brett said.

"Are you rendering me redundant?" Claudia joked. "How do you know so much about her?"

"It's possible I developed a crush on Nikki after I met her on a USO tour. She was a good diversion from reality when I was deployed."

"Got it. Between the two of us, it sounds like she's in good hands. Behave yourself."

The call ended, leaving Brett alone with his thoughts. He did a mental rundown of what he knew about Nicki. She was a notoriously private person and she was rarely seen with an entourage. He remembered reading about a home invasion in Beverly Hills a few years ago. A man had slipped through security and made it as far as her kitchen where Nikki subdued him by herself. She'd left California for several months and stopped taking leading roles after that.

Was this sudden appearance in Charleston a result of similar trouble?

Curious, he found a podcast that covered Hollywood dirt and gossip. He had just finished the most recent episode—and no mention of Nikki—when he reached the exit for the resort. Tourism in Charleston had boomed in recent years, thanks in part to the Ellington family, outside investors and a plethora of articles about what a lovely place Charleston was.

Personally he preferred the quirkiness of Folly Beach over the luxury that oozed from the rental mansions and the resort on the Isle of Palms.

But this wasn't about him.

Palmetto trees lined the drive to the resort and gave way to a circular drive that offered an easy view of those coming and going. He made a note to check into less obvious ways to get Nikki in and out. Pulling to a stop, he handed his key and a tip to the valet standing by and grabbed his bag from the back.

He went inside to the front desk, impressed by the seasonal, if unnecessary, fire crackling near a seating area on the other side of the wide room. He smiled to himself, taking in the upscale, flawless decor, and fresh flowers throughout. Though each item had surely been meticulously selected and placed, the welcoming hospitality and Charleston charm remained.

The man who checked him in and assigned him a room informed him all charges had been covered. "There is a note here for you, sir," he added. "Your party asked you to call upon your arrival." He slid a card across the countertop with a phone number.

"Thanks," Brett replied. The number began with a California area code that he recognized because he had friends there who frequently invited him out to surf.

He took the wide central stairs from the lobby to the second level. From there he walked down the hall and up to the third floor. The thick carpeting swallowed the sound of his footsteps. Finding his room, he stepped inside and turned on the light. He had a superb view of the ocean and the sky getting primed for a gorgeous sunset. He walked out on the balcony to listen to the rollers meeting the sand.

It was low tide and only a few resort guests were out on the stretch of private beach. He noticed more people gathered at the hotel bar tucked between the beach access boardwalk and the hotel pool. According to the resort map, the resort's signature restaurant was located behind the bar, boasting an unobstructed panoramic view of the ocean.

Brett didn't bother to unpack. That wasn't his speed. His time in the military had trained him to be ready to move in or out of any situation in an instant. From the balcony, he dialed the number on the card, praying it wouldn't go directly to Nikki. He wasn't sure he was ready to talk to the woman he'd crushed on from afar.

It didn't really matter that he'd never had a chance, mainly because she didn't know he existed. The woman had been born out of his league. Still, something about Nikki's fresh face and effervescent energy on-screen continued to tempt him to dream about the impossibility of real-life happiness.

CHAPTER 3

"Was that him?" Nikki asked when Hank finished the short phone call and returned her phone.

"It was," Hank replied.

"I didn't hear you tell him he wasn't needed." She caught the flash of a frown on Sadie's face, but she couldn't work up any regret. Nikki was still miffed that Hank had requested someone local to handle her security. Someone he hadn't met personally and was only vetted by another person she didn't know.

Needing a bodyguard was bad enough when she was sure about the person's background and professional ethics. She did *not* want to take a chance on a bodyguard no one could truly vouch for. A bodyguard Haynes—or someone else—might bribe into betraying her.

"An hour ago, over appetizers, you were agreeable," Sadie reminded her. "One glass of wine shouldn't give you that much of a bravado boost."

"It isn't about bravado and you know it." She purposely sipped from her water glass.

"What I know is, you shouldn't be alone. Think about the production. There are children involved."

Nikki gaped at her friend, shocked by the low, but accurate blow. She started to apologize when Sadie's face lit up as she looked past Nikki. "Too late," she whispered. "I do believe help has arrived." She nudged her husband who gave a nod at someone she couldn't yet see.

Hank must have shared some bio or headshot for this bodyguard of convenience. With his wife, but not her. Tamping down her frustrations, Nikki silently vowed to only need this stranger long enough for one of Hank's men to arrive and replace him.

"Hank Patterson?"

Hank stood, extending his hand. Sadie followed suit.

"Brett Robinson. A pleasure to meet you both."

His voice flowed over her, mellow with a confident undercurrent that reminded her of Hank. Then he stepped into view and she was struck by a strange sense that they'd met before. He extended his hand to her. "I'm Brett."

"Nikki," she managed. "Please join us," she added,

remembering her manners before things could get really awkward.

Although his voice soothed her, his striking features had the opposite effect, making her restless. He was tall, and the thick, dark waves of his hair were styled back from his face. A sexy scruff shaded his square jawline and to her astonishment, her fingers tingled with an urge to trace those short whiskers. His eyes, framed by dark straight eyebrows, were an icy, pale blue. She was immediately drawn to his casual style and easy grace as he moved around to her right. In his red polo shirt, khaki slacks, and deck shoes, he didn't resemble the bulked up bodyguards she was used to dealing with.

He met her appraisal head on, with a cool smile and she found herself a little star struck by him. Impressed. Is this how her fans felt when they stared at her either at a loss for words or gushing compliments?

Yes, she'd been born to Hollywood royalty and naturally blessed with features directors and fans appreciated. But she'd worked her way up, invested in herself by learning her craft in front of and behind the camera. In truth, she wasn't any different from any other hard-working, focused person, dedicated to their work.

"Nikki," he said, his voice snapping her out of her reverie. "It's good to see you again."

He sat down in the empty chair and suddenly they

were two couples out for the evening. She couldn't decide how if that was good or bad. Or if it even mattered. Then his words registered. What was he playing at? She didn't know him. Did he have reason to believe that Haynes was watching?

She refused to look. Refused to panic. They were surrounded by people and Hank was here. What could Haynes accomplish tonight?

"I won't embarrass either of us," Brett continued with a smile, "by telling you exactly how many days have passed since our last meeting."

She shook her head. "What are you talking about?" She'd never been a fan of games. There was enough pretending on the job. In real life she craved honesty and sincere connections.

The waitress came over and Brett ordered a local beer. Clearly the man was familiar with the area. Maybe they'd met in passing the last time she'd visited. As the waitress walked off, Brett smiled again and something deliciously warm tightened low in Nikki's belly.

"Thank you," he began. "We met during one of your USO tours. You graciously posed for pictures with every last one of us. A friendly ray of sunshine in a harsh situation. I've never forgotten it."

"Oh that makes a lot of sense," she said, relaxing at the logical explanation for the familiarity she couldn't shake. "I don't mean to be rude by not remembering you specifically." Although it was awful that she'd managed to forget this man's captivating... eyes. Who was she kidding? The whole man captivated her.

Still, she didn't *know* him. He couldn't stay. She opened her mouth to tell him he wasn't needed, but he spoke first.

"Is this your first trip to Charleston?" he asked.

"No." She reached for her wine and stopped, better to stick with the water. What should she do with her hands? She tucked them into her lap. "I made a couple of preliminary visits while I was working out the contract for this production. I've also visited the Greenville area.

"South Carolina offers a bountiful variety," Brett said. Thankfully, he shifted his attention to ask Hank and Sadie the same question.

While Hank explained the family's decision to make a mini-vacation out of Sadie's business trip, Nikki focused on finding her lost composure.

Not in time. That gaze returned to her. "And how would you like me to proceed?" he asked.

"Honestly, I'd prefer if you left."

"Nikki!" Sadie scolded in a harsh whisper, breaking out the mom voice. "You need someone watching your back."

Nikki glared at her friend. "My apologies for any inconvenience or misunderstanding, Brett. She's right. I did agree to Hank's suggestion to bring someone in."

"Just not me?" he challenged with a spark in his eyes.

"Basically, that's right. I'm sure you're perfect. I mean, I'm sure you're competent." Feeling her cheeks flaming, she was sure she should shut her mouth. She kept talking. "I've had security in the past and in general I do just fine and I'm much happier without anyone under foot."

"Understood," Brett said. He thanked the waitress when his beer arrived and confirmed that he would have a piece of the snapper Hank had caught, along with the rest of them. "I can handle things in a way that gives you plenty of room."

"How about all of the room?" she countered. "It's possible there isn't even a real problem." It wasn't entirely a lie. With her checkered past with both fans and staff, a little paranoia was warranted.

"Nikki," Hank warned.

Brett tilted his head, still all smiles. "You are a wonderful actress," he said. "But I have it on good authority I'm needed. People don't call me in for no reason." She started to protest, but he rolled right over her. "At the end of the day, it is your call." He leaned close and she caught a whiff of sunshine on his clothing. "Can I at least have dinner before I get back on the road?"

"Of course. It will be a pleasure."

He was too reasonable, and far too attractive. Hank and Sadie were clearly on his side. This wasn't the time or place for a scene. She'd learned her lesson about public displays of temper in her teens.

Throughout the meal, she let the three of them carry the conversation about the upcoming holidays and traditions and sightseeing the Patterson's wanted to do in the days ahead. When asked, she chimed in about The Nutcracker, and steered the conversation toward the plans for the afterparty.

It was quickly obvious that Brett adored Charleston and knew the city as well or better than the tour guides she'd met on her earlier visits. While the conversation flowed and the sun set in a blaze of orange and indigo, Nikki's thoughts wandered. Why couldn't Haynes leave her alone? And who would he use, who would he turn against her for the promise of a few extra bucks during the holidays?

Trust had never been an easy commodity. Friends were fickle, happy to color the truth if it meant a quote in an article or a chance for their work or faces to be seen by her parents. Boys had often been interested only while she picked up the tab. All those chances to toughen up and it still hurt when she was betrayed.

Haynes had been like that. Not a friend or confidant, but a peer she had respected until he abused his authority by suggesting sexual favors was the only way she could advance. She still regretted not reporting him immediately. Instead, she'd doubled down and proven him wrong through her solid work ethic.

Sadie reached across the table and squeezed her hand. "We need to get back upstairs for Emma, but you two should definitely chat some more." The meaning was clear. If Nikki sent Brett away, Sadie would only insist he return.

"We're reading her a different Christmas story every night this month," Hank explained to Brett, as he helped his wife to her feet. "I think Sadie packed a suitcase just for stories."

Sadie gazed up her husband, her eyes twinkling. "I think it's more likely that extra suitcase was just for your boots," she teased.

Brett struck a worried look, asking Sadie, "Tell me he is not wearing cowboy boots on the beach."

"Not a chance I'll let him get away with that," she said. "The paparazzi would never let that go."

"Dinner's on us," Hank said. "Stay and enjoy yourselves as long as you like."

Nikki understood the optics here. To anyone nearby, the established couple was giving the new couple time to bond. It was an effective ploy, one she hoped wouldn't show up as online tabloid click-bait tomorrow.

They had to come to an agreement, but she didn't know where to start. It wasn't as if he was an employee she had to terminate. She liked him well enough as a person.

"Look," Brett began before she could say a word. "I know you don't want me here. I *can* be invisible."

"That won't be enough. Not after tonight." She started to elaborate when another waitress walked over with a glass of wine. "I didn't order this," Nikki said.

"No, it's from a fan sitting at the bar," she explained. "Should I take it back?"

"Yes." Brett twisted in his seat to get a view of the bar.

"No, no. It's fine." Nikki smiled. "Please pass along my thanks."

"Of course."

"You can't drink that." Thankfully, he kept his voice low. "Not under the circumstances."

"No one's ever tried to poison me." She smiled as if he'd said the most amusing thing. "It's always better to be gracious."

"This happens often?" he asked.

"Often enough. Usually there's a request involved. For an autograph or a picture."

Brett's expression was bland, but she saw the tension in his hands. "Do me a favor and don't drink it," he said. "We're not even sure if I'm on the job yet, but it would still wreck my reputation if you got hurt on my watch."

"I have to at least pretend to take a sip," she said under her breath. Reaching for the glass, she noticed the corner of the cocktail napkin was folded in, revealing a bit of writing underneath.

Surreptitiously she drew the note closer while lifting the glass to her lips. Expecting the typical request, the words scrawled on the napkin were positively vicious: *Get rid of him or I will*

The wine barely touched her lips before she set the glass back on the table. Fear gripped the back of her neck in a cold vise.

Under the table, Brett bumped his knee to hers. "Steady," he said. "Let me see it."

She hadn't realized she had the note balled up inside her fist. With an effort she uncurled her fingers and let him look. The only sign that he was affected was the slight tightening of his jaw.

"Let's walk a bit," he said. "Go ahead and bring the wine."

BRETT POCKETED the note and kept a tight leash on his temper as they left the restaurant, passing the bar on their way to the dimly-lit deck beyond. Who would send her such a note? From his quick review of her case, the man supposedly troubling her wasn't in it for a relationship. Was this note sender a new problem or just a new tactic?

"Did you recognize anyone at the bar," he said at her

ear. Beside him, she practically vibrated. With fear or fury? This wasn't the first time she had been threatened and she'd proven her ability to take care of herself.

He wanted to be her support. It was a natural instinct, but he suspected if he tried to embrace her right now she would fight him off. Staring out over the water, his hand barely touching hers where they rested on the railing, he asked, "Have you recognized anyone in the area since you've arrived?"

"N-no," she stuttered. "This kind of thing is exactly why I left California this month."

"So someone specific has been harassing you?"

"I'm Nicki Weston, someone is always harassing me," she muttered.

From another client that might have come off as a victim mentality. Not Nikki. She spoke with simple authority as if this was just a common life experience. The sun comes up, someone pesters her, the sun sets.

"I'm aware of how that sounds," she said. "Crazy, paranoid, narcissistic, even."

"Not from my view. What sounds crazy to me is drinking wine you didn't order and turning away help." He angled his body to block her from view of anyone at the bar. "Your response implies you know who sent the note."

She turned and set the wine glass on an empty table, untouched except for that first near sip. "I've traveled alone and with bodyguards," Nikki said. "This stuff still happens."

Her voice was a raw whisper and he heard the pain and a sense of helplessness that irritated him. He wanted to fix this, and everything else for her. "The kitchen invader story made the rounds. Doesn't seem like that's the only time you've had to protect yourself. Where did you learn?"

"I started with self-defense classes. When that wasn't enough, I systematically pulled back from public life."

"And yet someone managed to interfere with a nice evening."

"Right."

The tide was rolling in and the beach narrow, the dry path closer to the lights bleeding from the resort. "Why don't we take a walk and you can tell me more."

She stared at him, incredulous. "A walk in the dark? If I don't shove you into the ocean that note claims he will."

"I'll take my chances." Brett lifted his chin toward the water. "Come on. Tell me who wrote this and why."

"Who knows why?" She made a little growling sound in her throat as they started across the boardwalk protecting the sand dunes. "I think it's Gus Haynes," she said. "Although I haven't seen him and he's never made a personal threat like that."

At the bottom of the steps on the beach side of the walkway, he stopped and toed off his deck shoes, offering his arm for balance while she stepped out of her sandals. It fascinated him how she relaxed as they walked deeper into the shadows away from the resort.

"You don't know me, but I am very good at my job," he said. "You're the client and I want you to be comfortable with the protection plan."

"I'd feel better if Hank knew you."

Her confession surprised him, but it gave him some insight as well. "I was a Navy SEAL," he began. "Had to carve a new path when my vision was damaged during an operation. I can still see and shoot well, just not well enough to be on a team. Most importantly, based on my crash course in Nikki Weston, I cannot be bought off."

"Everyone says they have integrity. Until the price is right."

He hadn't expected so much cynicism from the woman who'd always been the epitome of friendly and bright. Leaning on his expectations, based on a random public encounter, wasn't fair to either of them. He changed tactics before she relegated him to long-distance surveillance.

"How long have you known Sadie and Hank?"

"Sadie and I met when she first came to Hollywood," Nikki replied. "She is one of my truest friends."

"Never let you down?"

"Not once," she admitted. "I'm well aware she's worried about me, but bringing in a stranger to be my bodyguard isn't the answer."

He could feel her tensing up again, despite the lull of the ocean and the velvet sky full of stars. "What would be the answer?"

She stopped short and tilted her head back to study him, moonlight caressing her face. "I used to dream of being a normal kid, the easy-going girl next door everyone liked." She sighed, the sound sad and wistful. "Only movie scripts have made that possible."

"And playing that girl next door on the big screen only exacerbated the problem in real life?"

"Correct."

"Seems like a pretty sad half existence," he observed. "You do know you're just as entitled to the life you want as everyone else."

"Now you're a therapist too?" She chuckled, walking on down the beach. "Does everyone else include people who send me bossy ugly notes with free drinks?"

"Not in my opinion," Brett said. "Can I ask how old you are?"

"That wasn't covered in your crash course?" She stopped once more, wandering closer to the water's edge. "Every detail of my life is internet fodder."

"I know you were born on Christmas Day, never bothered checking the year." Taking a chance, he caught her hand and kept them moving, pleased when she didn't pull away. Movement would make her more of a challenge for anyone watching them. "Admiring you, hell crushing on you doesn't require memorizing your personal history."

"Then that makes you one of a kind," she said. "And disqualifies you from the fandom."

He chuckled, considering that the highest praise. "That one of a kind sets me apart from typical body-guards too."

The low and sexy sound of her laughter rippled over him in the darkness, stirring up desires that had nothing to do with job performance.

"You are confident, I'll give you that," she said. "Tell me how you'll do the job differently from typical bodyguards."

He pounced on the opening. "First of all, I'm the picture of discretion because I work alone. Almost alone. I have a technical assistant who is top notch," he said. "She watches my six and can deliver situa-tional intel in real time. She analyzes background and tracks people down. If Haynes is in South Carolina, she'll turn over every rock until she finds him."

"He's here," Nikki said.

"Let me be your buffer. Your shield. I can also be your witness, which will help when you press charges."

"It sounds good." She tossed her hair out of her face. "Above all I want the production to be protected. Hank spoke with theater security earlier today. And although it sounds good, no matter what happens, I can't press charges."

"Why not?" he asked, baffled.

"When I press charges or file a complaint, I'm seen as the paranoid diva. Your tech assistant should check out how easily people have avoided penalties for stalking and harassing me."

"Hasn't anyone told you not to read your own press?"

She laughed, the sound dark and bitter. The wind caught her hair and he brushed it away from her face in a move that was far too familiar between two people who had just met. But this close, it was impossible not to notice the effect he had on her. It made him bold and gave him another idea.

"You seem like a very nice man, and I thank you for your service."

"Uh-huh. Don't bother trying to let me down easy."

"I'm trying to make sure you don't get caught up where you don't belong. Whether you're nearby or watching me from some remote location, notes like that will still arrive."

"You know what I hear when you say things like that?"

"Do tell."

"I hear a woman who has been let down too many times. But if Hank and his wife, *your friend*, are worried about you and notes like this are inter-rupting your private time and distracting you from the job, you need someone on your side to deal with it head-on."

She slid away from him, her arms crossed over her middle, sandals swinging from her finger. If they weren't on the beach he imagined he would hear her toe tapping impatiently. "Hank told me the resort has its own security."

"And you can bet I'll be talking with them about how that note still found you." Why was she being so stubborn? Did she have a death wish or had drama just become a way of life? "Is there someone signifi-cant in your personal life?" he asked. "Boyfriend, ex-boyfriend, secret affair?"

"No," she replied, too quickly.

Her gaze dropped to her feet and her toes curled into the damp sand. A strange vulnerability swirling around her. Before he could second-guess himself, he wrapped her into a hug. She was stiff in his embrace, but she didn't fight him off. After a moment, her body relaxed and her head dropped to his shoulder.

Heaven. She felt so perfect in his arms, he nearly let go. "You need help he said. Give me forty-eight hours before you kick me to the curb and call me useless."

"What if he gets past you and hurts someone in the cast?"

"He's not after the cast," Brett pointed out.

"What if you get hurt?" she asked.

"It sure wouldn't be the first time," he said. "I heal. Military service isn't nearly as kind and gentle as people think."

"Stop joking." She backed out of his arms. "Men leave me. Women betray me. I'm betting that in forty-eight hours, you'll be long gone too."

"I'll take that bet," he said. "What's the wager? Money or something better?"

She rolled her eyes. "Guess that depends on what you think is better than money."

"How about this," he began. "You cooperate with my plan to protect you for the forty-eight hours. If we haven't resolved this by then you owe me a real people date."

"What is a real people date?"

"The full girl-next-door treatment," he replied. "I'll make the plans, pick you up and show you a great time."

"And if you're gone before then, I suppose *that's* my prize."

Her mulish expression made him want to smile. She was intrigued by him, even if she wouldn't admit it. "That and you get your money back," he replied.

"I suppose this isn't the time to mention that Hank is footing the bill?"

"Wherever the money comes from, if I'm gone, you have the pride of being right," he said. And in his experience pride didn't keep anyone warm at night.

Whoops. Now that was in his head: the chance to keep her warm at night. A fantasy so far-reaching he couldn't really enjoy it. "Any conditions or are we agreed?

"I want to hear your plan first."

"Smart woman," he said. Placing his hand lightly at the small of her back, he guided her towards the resort. "Initially I thought I would need your schedule and names and contact information for the people you work with every day."

"And now?"

"I'll still need that, but the note that came with the wine and the altered postcard on your car were personal threats. More dangerous in some ways, but simpler for me in others."

"Simpler? No way."

"If it is Haynes, he clearly wants you alone. Let me wreck his plan by playing the role of your new boyfriend. You're normally very private and tend to avoid the public, but with this Nutcracker production you'll be more visible, right?

"Yes." She nodded, her gaze on the resort up ahead. "I have to be. My only comfort is that Charleston is much smaller than Hollywood."

"And friendlier," he added. "Charleston is also the perfect place for a romantic holiday getaway. No one in your fan base will think twice about your new boyfriend showing up here for the first time."

"Is there an alternative?"

It was a blow to the ego, but he was beginning to think he wasn't her type in any sense of the word. Fake or not, being rejected by the world's idea of the perfect woman cut deep.

"Sure. Typical bodyguard tactics, very official from the sunglasses to a dark suit. Lots of intimidating hovering over your every step. Based on what I've seen, I'm not giving you the stakeout from afar option."

"Because you had a crush on me."

"No. Because I know my job whether you approve or not." They'd reached the walkway that bridged the sand dunes. He shoved his feet back into his shoes, ignoring the gritty sand and she slipped back into her sandals, the heels lifting her an inch or two. Lights from the bar spilled out, making them visible to anyone bothering to look their way.

He smoothed another wind-blown lock of her silky hair away from her cheek. "Make your decision. Boyfriend or bodyguard?"

She stared up at him, eyes wide and lips parted slightly and he realized what a talented actress she was. Her breath hitched and she licked her lips as she leaned close. "Boyfriend," she whispered, right against his lips.

His response was reflex, his hands learning the dip of her waist as he pulled her closer and kissed her back. It was a little like falling out of a plane, those first breath-stealing seconds before the parachute opened.

He would gladly ride this sensation forever. She was hot and sweet, that generous mouth responsive, sparking cravings inside him for so much more as she linked her hands behind his neck. How did they do this in the movies?

When she eased back and he was mesmerized by her plumped lips and sparkling eyes. She knew what was rioting through him, had counted on creating that reaction.

Had he just gotten himself fired?

"I have an early day tomorrow," she said, her hands toying with his hair.

"What time should I pick you up?"

She frowned.

"I'll drive you to the theater," he clarified. He shifted his eyes to the resort and back to her, hoping she'd catch his meaning. If this was her choice, they had to start the boyfriend charade right now. "You promised to let me watch you work, remember?

Her brilliant smile lit him up inside. "Of course, I remember." She peered up at him from under her lashes. "How about you bring breakfast to the room at seven."

"Sounds perfect."

They didn't talk on the way upstairs to her room and he was grateful not to be tested when his mind was a jumble and his body was insisting she was into him. At her door, he made sure his number was in her phone and then he touched his lips lightly to her cheek.

"Sweet dreams," he said. "I'm only two doors down if you need me." He waited until she was inside and he heard the deadbolt turn. Walking away from her was the hardest thing he'd done since leaving the Navy.

When he was back in his room he called Claudia with the update.

"I expected to hear from you hours ago," she scolded without any real heat.

"Yeah, I've been pleading my case," he admitted. "Independent is just the tip of the iceberg with Nikki. She doesn't want the intrusion of personal protection."

"But she's okay with Haynes stalking her? Did you come to an agreement?" Claudia asked.

"Eventually," he assured her. "I negotiated for forty-eight hours, handling things my way. I'll be playing her boyfriend." He ignored the guffaw on the other end of the line. "Not ideal but far better than vacating the job or watching from a distance. This guy is escalating."

Claudia made a humming sound. "You know, Brett, it's hard to get a read on what you're thinking about this case. Can you be objective?"

"It's hard to get a read on her," he admitted. "And yes." He rubbed at the back of his neck, thinking of

Nikki's touch. "Someone sent over a glass of wine while we were getting acquainted after dinner. It was accompanied by a nasty little note telling her to get rid of me."

Claudia whistled. "So that's why you went for the boyfriend role."

Her phrasing reminded him of the kiss and how well Nikki managed the scene. "Fastest way I know to draw him out," Brett said. "She didn't recognize anyone around the bar who might have sent the drink and note, but she's convinced Haynes is behind it."

"I've only started digging," Claudia said. "We'll find him."

"It would really help to have some quick background on her. Things a boyfriend would know. Like how old she is and what she likes for breakfast."

"She'll be thirty in a few days," Claudia replied. "That's all the freebies you get, Romeo. I have real work to do for this case. Check out Instagram and do a search for interviews. Or you could just take the easy road and ask Sadie."

"Fine." He wasn't going to sleep tonight anyway. "Any word on Tyler?" he asked, not quite ready for the silence of his room.

"You don't like the way I do things?"

He recognized the teasing tone. "Just the opposite. You're too perfect for me."

"True enough," she said. "You know the agency

doesn't believe in transparency. All I know is Tyler isn't available. Feel free to grill him all you want when he's back on duty."

Brett didn't want to grill him at all. He just wanted to make sure the kid was okay. He hoped it was a vacation. During their last case Tyler had been distracted and easily frustrated. Usually the kid managed a hundred things simultaneously without breaking a sweat, but something had been weighing on his mind.

"Are you doing anything special for the holidays?" he asked, inexplicably reluctant to get off the phone.

"Got the family thing all set at the farm," she replied. "My sister and her boyfriend will join us. Don't take this the wrong way, but I'd rather not hear your voice after Christmas Eve, is that clear?"

"Yes ma'am."

She snorted. "What about you and the new celebrity girlfriend?"

Brett thought about their wager. Odds were good, assuming he caught Haynes red-handed in the next day or two, that she could spend a worry-free Christmas and birthday with her friends. Not him. He wasn't really her boyfriend despite how much that kiss rocked him.

The whole reason for his work, his sole purpose here, was to resolve difficult and threatening situations so a person could get back to living their best life. But in Nikki's case he was afraid that she had spent too much time hiding and would never get back to living fully, no matter who they caught or how they meted out justice.

"Brett? Brett? Damn, I lost the signal," Claudia muttered.

"No, I'm here. Got distracted with breakfast research," he lied.

"Get some rest," she instructed. "I'll have more information for you in the morning."

"I'll do that," he said. "Thanks for the assist."

But after a few minutes online he realized he couldn't rest until he figured out what was real and what was internet hearsay about her breakfast choices? Maybe he should just call Sadie. Fortunately he checked the time before he made that call. No way would he risk waking the little girl or her parents.

Instead of taking another deep dive into Nikki's social media history for pictures of smoothies or overnight oats, he went downstairs to the resort kitchen. After a little sweet talking with the overnight staff, and explaining his honorable intentions, he was given a peek at what Nikki usually ordered for room service breakfast.

He made several selections, adjusting her original order, adding a tip and specific instructions to let him take care of the delivery.

On his way back upstairs, he stopped at the front desk to speak with security. After introducing himself and dropping Hank's name, he showed the man on duty the note Nikki had received and asked to look at any surveillance footage.

Brett and the security officer sifted through the video of the evening. They saw the man order the drink and write the note, but they couldn't get a good look at his face. It was as if the man knew where the cameras were and how to avoid them. And he'd paid cash, so that possible identifier was a bust as well.

Brett thanked the security officer and headed out. Too much to hope that he'd get a bead on Haynes so quickly. Cases were rarely that easy. And although he didn't want Nikki in danger, he was actually looking forward to spending some time with her.

At just past midnight, the bar was still open so Brett headed out and interviewed the bartender about the man who'd ordered the wine for Nikki. He got a good description and Brett sent that on to both Claudia and Hank by text. The more people they had looking for this guy, the sooner they could confirm if it was Haynes or someone new.

He wasn't going to let anyone wreck her Christmas or her birthday.

On the way back to his room, he detoured down the hallway to the kiosk where snacks, toiletries, books, and other items were on sale. He wasn't exactly hungry but he was restless. Deciding it was a perfect night for chocolate, he reached for a candy bar when he heard the squeak of a shoe on the flooring behind him.

His response to the sound saved him a concussion. Or worse. He turned just as a man swung a fire extinguisher at him. The improvised weapon landed hard on the back of his shoulder and neck instead of his skull, though it was enough to leave him seeing stars. The fire extinguisher hit the floor with a clang and his attacker fled, Brett stumbling after him.

Security and the front desk clerk came running, responding to the commotion, but it was too late. The man was gone, escaping through a side door that led to the parking lots. Although they reviewed camera angles again, Brett had to concede this round.

CHAPTER 4

Early the next morning, Nikki waited until she heard a knock on her door. She even paused to check the peephole to make sure it was Sadie and not some idiot with a glass of wine. On previous mornings she would've met her friend down on the beach, but last night's note made her cautious.

She was struggling just to make small talk, her mind darting between the wild change in Haynes's tactics and kissing Brett. She was happier dwelling on kissing Brett. Her new fake bodyguard had featured in her dreams when she finally fell asleep last night and the workout wasn't the only thing increasing her heart rate.

"You're mad at me about Brett aren't you?" Sadie demanded when they were well away from the resort. "Maybe I overstepped, springing him on you at dinner, but I am really worried."

"Not mad," Nikki said. "I'm worried too," she admitted. "After you and Hank left the table someone sent over a drink. And a note."

"Oh, my god. How bad?"

"Different," she said. "And before you make me say it, yes I was glad Brett was there." She had to pause for breath. "The note told me to get rid of Brett or the sender would do it."

Sadie swore. "Did you see him?"

"No." That was driving her crazy, knowing it had to be Haynes and yet not seeing him when these things happened. "But he had to be there right?"

Sadie frowned. "He's paid people to do the dirty work before. I'm sure Brett is on it."

"I'm sure," she agreed.

"I'm glad you're keeping him on," Sadie said as they turned back.

"Yeah, about that." Nikki glanced around, but they were alone. "We decided to handle this situation like a new couple."

Sadie's eyebrows arched up over her sunglasses, her lips rounding into a perfect 'o'. "That has all kinds of potential, my friend."

"He's a professional," Nikki said. A professional who kissed like the real deal. "You need to know the truth so you don't get wild ideas. This is just the safest approach."

"Ideas? Me?" Sadie asked with exaggerated innocence. "Just remember happily-ever-afters do happen."

If only. "What worked for you and Hank doesn't work for everyone," Nikki reminded her. Her own romantic past was fraught with deception and disappointment. Even pretending with Brett felt risky to her emotional health. But there was no doubt it was necessary.

They walked along the beach, on the same general path she had taken with him last night, and Nikki turned the conversation to business. Both women had pet projects they wanted to get off the ground. "Will you and Hank head out to Georgia today?" Nikki asked.

"That's the plan," Sadie replied. "We're going to take a look at two different locations after we meet with the film office. The three of us won't be back until late tonight."

"You'll have a great time." Nikki gave her a hug as they parted ways at the resort.

The butterflies in her stomach were a pleasant surprise. Brett would be in her room in a few minutes. When was the last time she'd been fluttery about a man? Most of the time caution ruled, muting attraction and anticipation before it really took hold.

She hurried to clean up and get dressed before Brett arrived with breakfast. The ocean breeze had put a rosy glow in her cheeks, so she only applied sunscreen, mascara and lip gloss. Pulling the tie from her hair, she brushed it out and wound it back up into a bun, ready for rehearsal.

The knock sounded on the door promptly at seven, just as she slipped into her tennies. Checking her reflection she decided it was the right blend of producer-at-work and potential couple time. One thing she'd learned early in life as the Weston daughter and heir, was to always dress the part.

Making sure it was Brett, she opened the door. The aromas from the tray in his hands hit her first. He'd brought something savory and hot. Bacon. Hopefully enough to share. Not that she didn't start many of her days with a power smoothie, but she was a woman who valued good food. If he'd brought something hearty for himself and a cold smoothie for her, she'd fire him.

Or try.

Her knees felt weak. He was sexier this morning than he'd been last night. His hair damp from a shower, he looked amazing in pressed khaki slacks and a button down shirt, with a dark brown belt and oiled boat shoes.

"Good morning," he said. "Can I come in?"

"Of course." Embarrassed she'd been caught staring, she backed up. "Is this the Carolina boyfriend look?" she asked.

"I can change if this doesn't work for you. It just seemed neutral enough to go anywhere today."

Oh, his look was definitely working for her. She

appreciated a man who knew how to dress. Now to figure out if he knew how to eat. He crossed the room as if he'd been here a dozen times and unloaded the tray to the table.

He'd brought a muffin, a wrapped breakfast sandwich, a tall cup that was surely the smoothie, and two larger plates. Then he upended a small bag, and syrup packets and butter fell across the table.

"How much do you think I eat?" she asked.

"Does it matter? You have a fridge for leftovers." He tipped his head toward the appliance tucked in to the cabinet. "Besides, after your morning run I wasn't sure if you'd feel green or if you'd be starving."

"Starving," she said. "And we have a big day ahead."

He smiled. "My grandmother always said fresh air and sunshine would work up an appetite."

She felt her lips curling in response. "I have to agree with her." How was she supposed to resist a boyfriend-bodyguard who loved his grandma?

He removed the cover from one plate, revealing an egg scramble with cheese, slices of crisp bacon, and a pancake. The other plate was a ham and veggie omelet with a biscuit, sausage patties, and a side of gravy. "Ladies choice," he said.

"Nice. All my carbs in one place," she joked, taking a seat and pulling the plate with bacon in front of her.

He handed her silverware wrapped in a cloth napkin.

"If you ordered room service, why not let them serve?"

"They offered to bring it up," he said. "But I wanted to do the honors.

"Like a good boyfriend?" He was so cute. And tempting her on every front.

"Just like that," he responded, matching her tone.

He chose the breakfast sandwich. "Mind if I make myself a cup of coffee?"

"Go right ahead," she said. "Make yourself at home."

With a silly lift of his eyebrows, he walked to the single-cup coffee maker and helped himself. "Can I make one for you?"

"Yes, please." She couldn't fault his manners. In fact she really could get used to this kind of treatment.

"How do you take your coffee?" he asked when the first cup finished brewing.

But she was already halfway to the refrigerator. "Heavy cream," she replied. "Just a spoonful makes me feel special. Please don't tell anyone," she added. "The tabloids would have a field day and they'd attack me from all angles."

"Death by vegan?"

"That's just one possibility," she said. Taking the cup he offered, she poured sparingly from the carton of cream. "Only one cup a day like this, then black if I need more caffeine."

"You don't have to justify anything to me." He clearly meant it. "If it makes you happy, what else matters?"

She would probably sound like a ninny if she told him how much she appreciated those words. In her line of work and in an era when fans and critics had constant access, every little movement was hyper analyzed, judged, and usually found lacking by someone.

She sipped slowly. This was one indulgence she insisted on savoring every day. "I know it looks like I lead a charmed life," she said, once she finished her coffee and returned to her breakfast. "And seriously, my complaints are few compared to others."

"You're saying you do charity work and pump up local community theater out of guilt?"

His question startled her. The man had done his homework overnight. No one she'd employed as security had done that before. "Is this a boyfriend thing or is your agency that thorough?" she asked.

"Call it professional pride." He finished off his sandwich and wiped his fingers and lips. "No matter how it looks on the outside, knowing what matters to you makes it easier for me to do the actual protecting."

She might actually enjoy these next few days.

"Should I assume you've reviewed my schedule as well?"

"You should." He grinned at her as he sliced away a chunk of the omelet and put it on his plate. "I'm happy to go running with you tomorrow."

She couldn't suppress a smile. "You don't think Sadie qualifies as a bodyguard?"

"I'm sure Hank has taught her how to protect herself. She isn't my concern. You are."

It was tempting to bask in that intensity, but she'd been caught staring once already this morning. "At the risk of bruising your professional pride, I need that time with Sadie. It is a private beach."

"And an exclusive resort," he said, rolling his shoulder.

He didn't have to say the rest. They were both aware he was referring to that stupid note. She sighed and took another bite of her breakfast, her gaze on the view beyond the balcony where waves scurried up the beach.

"This ocean is so different from the Pacific," she mused. "Everything on this side of the country seems softer than the hard glitz of southern California."

"South Carolina is one of those places that sticks with you," he agreed.

She was discovering the same thing. "It's not my first visit, and I still can't tell if it's the people or the sunshine or the food, but every time I come I have a harder time leaving."

"You could live anywhere, right? Why not stay?"

It would be delightful. "Visibility is part of staying relevant," she replied. "Being seen, taking meetings." She sighed, weary of it all way too soon. "Some people thrive in it, but not me," she confessed, surprising herself. "Most of my fans want more interaction than I can comfortably give, but I try. And most fans know I'm not great with boyfriends."

"Then we'll give them something to talk about," he replied in a sexy Southern drawl that left her speechless. She fumbled about for any excuse not to talk and stuffed another bit of bacon into her mouth.

"We should probably review your plans," he said in his normal mellow voice. "First stop is the theater, right?" She nodded. "I won't get in your way, but I will be wandering, exploring weaknesses and access points.

"As long as you don't wander on stage, I'm good."

"No worries on that score." He grinned. "I'm a behind-the-scenes type."

He had the looks to be in front of a camera, but she kept the compliment to herself. "Makes two of us," she said. "I prefer to let others shine these days."

"Why is community theater so important to you?"

"Because it's raw and clean." She got up and started another cup of coffee for the drive to the theater. "Ego in a community theater is rarely damaging. People are there for the joy of it. The creativity employed due to budget and talent constraints inspires and rejuvenates me. And most of the time they're happy to see me," she finished with a self-deprecating chuckle. "I can go in and share some wisdom and encourage people. I love that."

"You're an inspiration," he stated.

The coffee finished and she poured it into a to-go cup.

Brett checked his watch. Not his phone. And the motion drew her eyes to his muscular forearms. She imagined the work that built up those strong wrist and hands. He was fit all over, but something about those hands made her feel safe and steady and he hadn't really touched her.

Aside from a kiss that sparked fantasies all night long.

Dragging her mind back to business, she gathered the dishes on the tray for housekeeping. It was her practice to be a good guest and she really didn't care for people to be in her room any more than necessary. Too many personal details had been leaked that way. Enough that she started to wonder if she had any personal details left.

Brett winced as he carried the tray to the hallway.

"Are you hurt?"

"Just sore," he said, donning his sunglasses. "You ready?"

She grabbed her purse and followed him into the hallway. Downstairs, his car was waiting out front and she sat back to enjoy the drive to the theater.

"I know what it's like when people want to get close to a hero," he said after he listened to a traffic update on his app. "They have an image in mind of what you should be."

She understood what he was getting at but she didn't think it was quite the same between his line of work and hers. It wasn't as if his face was plastered across media and tabloid sites as the most handsome Navy SEAL to ever serve the nation.

Although… *That was it!* "You've been on recruiting posters," she said, finally placing his face in her memory. "That's why you look so familiar."

He groaned and behind his dark sunglasses, she imagined he was rolling his eyes.

"I don't know whether to be flattered or offended," he said.

"Choose flattered, definitely." She patted his shoulder. "A Hollywood icon recognized you. How many sweet Carolina boyfriends can say the same?"

He bristled at the word sweet and she found herself delighted. "You know, you had the right idea with the boyfriend option."

"Did I?" he grumbled, adjusting his speed as they entered the tight streets of Charleston proper.

"Yes. I like it." At a stop light, she dared to lean over and kiss his cheek. This time, he hissed a little. "What's wrong?"

"Had a dust up last night while I was investigating who sent the note," he said, moving along with the traffic. "Not a big deal. Head of security is working on it today."

She wasn't buying the casual routine. "Haynes?"

"I assume so," Brett replied. "He tried to clobber me from behind. Fits the profile for Haynes, but he was dressed in a resort uniform. He bolted, avoiding all the best camera angles."

When he'd pulled into a parking space in the garage closest to the theater, she tugged at his shirt collar, cursing the colorful bruise. "I didn't mean to hurt you."

"You didn't." He gave her a smile that made her belly quiver and her pulse skip. "But feel free to touch me all you want."

She assumed the smile and flirty invitation was for show, but when she glanced around, no one was looking at them. Like the perfect Southern gentleman he had clearly been raised to be, he came around to open her door.

Together, they walked hand-in-hand out of the garage and down the block and it felt completely natural. She wasn't sure if it was just being with him that distracted her from any curious onlookers or if no one voiced any recognition because he was close.

She had worked hard to cultivate a private life, away from public view. Her last two relationships had ended because she refused more outrageous dates and outings at popular spots. She did the group thing with friends, but dates were completely behind closed doors.

But she couldn't dwell on any of that now. This was the last day to iron out any kinks in the performance. Tomorrow would be dress rehearsals and the day after marked the first of five nearly sold-out performances.

Then it would be Christmas. She would be thirty years old. She planned to celebrate with a beach and mimosas. After Christmas morning with the Patterson's of course.

"Ready?" he asked as they walked up the steps to the front doors.

"I should be asking you that question. Once the word boyfriend starts circulating…"

"I'll handle it," he promised.

He held the door open for her and she felt yet another flutter. There were times when she was such a girl. Too bad she could never let it show. Brett stirred up feminine tendencies she actually wanted to indulge. To savor like her morning coffee and cream. She actually missed the touch of his hand as she walked inside and she reached for him as soon as he joined her.

The theater manager, Mary Simms, met her first thing and Nikki introduced Brett. As she'd thought, boyfriend had Mary's eyebrows lifting with speculation. "He'll be wandering, if that's okay," Nikki said.

"Fine by me," Mary replied with a wink. "Per

yesterday's adjustment, we do have more security on hand today. And the reporters will be here at noon for your interview."

She'd forgotten all about that. "Great. I'm looking forward to it." As Mary left for the next task on her long to-do list, Nikki turned back to Brett. "It's going to be pretty intense for the next few hours," she warned.

"For both of us, he agreed, leaving no doubt that he would also be working to find any sign of the man who shouldn't even be on this side of the country.

He walked with her backstage and she pulled out her phone. "I drafted an email last night. It's my full history with Haynes. And some instances with others as well. In case it helps. What's your email address?" She entered it and hit send. "There you go."

His phone chimed a moment later. "Thank you. That couldn't have been easy."

His sincerity set her back on her heels and she didn't know what to say. She was shocked he understood so well. Maybe that insight came with being a bodyguard and she'd just never had the right kind of interested person on her side.

"So." She smiled up at him as the cast started filtering in. "Do I say break a leg or just give you a kiss for luck?" she asked.

"Rather have the kiss." He winked and pulled her in close to his heat and strength, but he kept the contact respectful.

Still, she was flushed as she retreated to her meeting with the set director.

WHILE NIKKI WAS MOVING dancers and set pieces around, Brett took a seat and reviewed her email. She had provided a brief rundown of troublesome people in her recent past. It jived with what Claudia had found, but having her personal account was better. Although it was a fairly dispassionate review, there were names to research.

He wished she could've told him in person, but it was good to have it in writing and much easier to forward to Claudia.

Rather than call and be overheard, he sent his assistant a text. Hopefully by now she would know if Haynes had actually made the trip to South Carolina. There had to be some reason Haynes had fixated on Nikki. Claudia would find it.

His job was dealing with the immediate safety of the client.

The music stopped abruptly and the dancers turned as Nikki stepped out onto the stage, her movements so graceful and fluid he couldn't watch anything else. Couldn't think of anything else. It was easy to see how she captivated audiences around the world. And now it was like the perfect Christmas present.

"Do what you love and you'll never work a day in your life," he said under his breath. This certainly didn't feel like work right now.

According to the schedule she would be in and around the stage area for at least another hour. With so many people around it was easy to be lulled into thinking she was safe. To be fair, she hadn't faced any trouble here, other than feeling like Haynes was watching.

He took a walk through the theater, confirming security personnel were here and on station. No one lurked in the seating area who didn't have a reason to be there. He checked on her backstage, and then walked back to the front of the house. The theater manager was greeting the reporter who had the honor of interviewing Nikki in less than an hour. Up in the lighting booth everything was fine and secure.

Returning to his seat, Brett used the free time to make plans for the afternoon. He knew he would win the bet, but for the job, being seen out and about as a couple could push Haynes to make a mistake.

At last a text message came back from Claudia that all but confirmed Nikki's suspicions. Haynes had not been seen in California since early December. In the next message Claudia relayed that she was looking into any credit card records for flight or hotel bookings.

Suddenly, someone screamed backstage, a sound he'd never heard in any other performance of The

Nutcracker. Why in the hell had he promised not to hover?

He charged to the stage, taking the fastest route to the wings where he had last seen Nikki. Some red fluid flowed across the floor as if someone had opened the back door and tossed a bucket of blood inside. No one was down, so it couldn't be blood. The fluid had splashed a few of the dancers who'd been nearby. There was plenty of crying and the older dancers were trying to usher younger ones away, but his only concern was locating Nikki.

She rushed him, her eyes wide and wild, her face pale, and her hands curled into fists. She looked braced for battle and he caught her close to his chest, keeping her from charging through the mess.

The theater manager and assistant director were right behind her. "Are you okay? Is everyone all right?"

She nodded. "No one's hurt."

For a split-second he thought she'd let him comfort her, instead she patted his chest and stepped back, a queen reclaiming charge of her domain.

"Mary called the police," she told him. "Anna," she addressed her assistant, "take them through end of day stretches and review any notes."

"What about the final scenes?" Anna asked.

"Forget it. The day is shot. They know what they're doing," she said, projecting so several people heard her. "Tell them I said they're fabulous. I'll handle this and the interview and pop in at the cookie party. We still have dress rehearsal tomorrow to hammer out any last concerns."

"You got it." Anna darted to the stage to carry out her orders.

"Nicely done," he said when it was just them and the theater manager backstage. "Can you tell me what happened?"

"I'm not sure," Nikki said. "I was focused on the stage." She took a breath. "The door opened, I only know that because the sunlight poured in."

"Followed by the blood," the manager said. "I was right there." She pointed. "The door flew open and then an object sailed through the air."

Nikki pushed at her hair, tightening the bun that had loosened from the active morning. "I turned just in time to see that." She flung a hand at the mess. "A ball or something. It hit the floor and splattered everywhere. Is it blood?"

"Doesn't smell like it," Brett replied. But it had caused damage that resembled the marked up post-card she'd shown Hank. "We'll let the police figure it out."

Nikki sniffed the air, moved closer to the mess. "Now that you mention it, it smells a little like wine."

She was right. Wine and the kind of washable paint kids used on craft projects. He remembered the smell from his grandmother's classroom. If this was wine, it was hard not to connect it to the note from last night.

Mary fumed, pacing around for a path to the door. "No one should have been back there. The door is unlocked during rehearsals and performances per the fire code, but I asked for a guard to be posted outside today."

Brett caught Nikki's gaze and read her like a book. She believed someone had been bribed. Again. This time he hoped she was right since the only logical alternative was someone injured out back. He wanted to get out there and investigate, but he wasn't about to leave Nikki alone.

"Did anything else come in?"

Both women shook their heads.

"No one said anything?"

Again, both women shook their heads. He shooed them back and moved closer to the mess, careful not to step in any of the spatter. With the lights up high, he noticed pieces that might be a latex balloon. "Seems like a long shot, just randomly lobbing this inside."

"It's not like we're doing Nutcracker in fur," Mary said, coming up beside him. "This looks like the type of thing activists tossed at people wearing fur coats. Minus the wine."

"True."

Mary's phone lit up and her eyes went wide. "I

forgot the reporter." When Nikki closed her eyes, she hurried to add. "I'll go smooth it over, no worries."

Brett cuddled Nikki close, offering the only comfort he had. "The police will figure it out," he promised. "I'm sorry I was out front."

"You were only following my request not to hover." She rested her head on his chest for a moment, but he tucked her behind him when the back door opened again.

Police entered, confirming the security officer was down in the alley.

Definitely escalating, Brett thought as he let them question Nikki. They were good with her, and with Mary too. To his astonishment, she named every dancer that was backstage at the time of the incident.

While the police worked the scene, Brett sent a text message to Claudia asking for a review of any security cameras with a view of the alley and nearby streets. It would take time, but Haynes couldn't evade every camera forever.

"Everyone is cooling down," Nikki was telling the police. "We're having a cookie party to celebrate. It's really the best place to corral the cast and ask your questions."

"How did you do that?" he asked under his breath as he escorted her to the front of the house for her interview. "You named every dancer."

"I've known this cast for 2 weeks now," she said.

"And I knew what scene we were on when it happened. No one is out sick so…" She shrugged.

"You're amazing."

"People matter to me." A blush stole over her cheeks as if the admission was far more than she'd meant to share.

"My assistant will find and follow any activity in the alley," he said. "Hopefully we will have a lead to share with the police."

"And until then?"

"I'll keep working our plan." He kissed her cheek and gave her a nudge toward the waiting reporter. "Go sell those last tickets," he said.

The smile she gave him was nothing short of brilliant, and filled him with a delicious spike of adrenaline. Although the reporter and makeup artist gave him the side eye as Nikki sat down to prepare for the interview, she didn't ask any personal questions.

Brett didn't want to start rumors, but he refused to let Nikki out of his sight. When the interview was over, she rushed over to the cookie party, to address the cast as promised.

Young and old, cast and crew alike were having a blast at the cookie party, making treats to take home for their families. She offered up praise, one bit of constructive criticism to the group as a whole, and reminded them of dress rehearsal report times tomorrow. She assured them the stunt backstage was random, and the police we're handling it.

"As far as we can tell," Nikki said, "this was an ill-advised prank, so don't sweat it. We have more important things to focus on."

He admired the way she settled the crowd, using all of her acting skills. She believed the stunt was related to her, that it was in fact, personal. He didn't think anyone else noticed the tremor in her hand when she waved farewell.

At least with rehearsal over for today, he had a chance to distract her for a little while.

CHAPTER 5

NIKKI HAD BEEN through some hard days at work through the course of her career. She knew what it was like to be scared, to be threatened, to be so tired she couldn't quite care about fear or threats. But stepping into the sunshine, her hand in Brett's, the reason for the abrupt end to the rehearsal faded. Almost as if it hadn't happened at all.

Her feet felt lighter, her heart too. "Thank you," she said. "You were rock solid, absolutely perfect in there."

"You're welcome."

He opened his mouth and she held up her hand. "I don't want to talk about it."

"Give me some credit." His lips tilted into that sexy grin. "I was going to tell you about our date."

"We don't have a date until the day after tomorrow."

"Call it an outing then. You haven't eaten since breakfast."

"Now?" Was he kidding? She wasn't dressed for any kind of a date or outing. She felt tired and gross and—

"If you'd rather, we can just call it lunch."

She laughed, surprising herself. "What did you set up?"

"Well if you're up for a walk, this Carolina boyfriend booked a picnic in the park, to be served with a side of history."

"Sounds like fun," she said, intrigued.

"Already hooked?" He bobbed his eyebrows. "That bodes well."

He pointed out various landmarks, even mentioned a ghost or two as they passed cemeteries. She was listening, but it was hard to focus on the past when the present company was so charming. This was just the type of thing she needed to wind down.

He paused at the next corner and pulled her out of the flow of tourists walking by. "Okay, I'm not sure what kind of a shopper you are, but I have a request."

"Name it." She was feeling remarkably agreeable.

"We're going to walk through the market, stop at *one* booth to pick up the picnic, and then we're leaving."

"This is a 'do not pass go, do not collect two hundred dollars' kind of thing?

"Exactly. If you want to shop, I can set that up with Hank and Sadie for another day."

The man was definitely a charmer. "I'll tell you a secret." She leaned in close. "Sadie and I have already torn up this place. Twice."

"Thank you for supporting the economy."

He held such a serious expression, she burst into giggles. *Giggles.* After what had just happened. The man was a miracle worker.

She nudged him when the crosswalk light flashed green. "Lead the way."

The market always tempted with so many items to explore, but she kept her word and didn't stop. He led her directly to a well-organized booth selling products from the Ellington Plantation. She'd learned on a previous visit to the area that the several branches of the extensive family owned and managed properties around town.

The woman tending the register at the booth beamed at Brett as she handed him a picnic hamper. Nikki would've offered to pay, but it seemed he'd handled that detail too. Exiting the market, he turned toward the park at the end of the peninsula.

"Figured we should make the most of clear weather," he said. He continued the tour guide routine as they navigated the sidewalks with ease. Informative and amusing, he shared all kinds of details about past and present Charleston that teased her imagination.

When they reached the park that spanned a wide

space between the stunning mansions of East Bay Street on one side and the harbor on the other, he found a spot for them under the wide limbs of a live oak tree. Pulling a blanket from the hamper, he spread it out for the two of them.

"You don't miss a trick," she said, thoroughly impressed.

"Full service package," he joked. "It's a Carolina thing."

Her mind went straight to the gutter, and she barely kept her eyes above his belt. "What did you order?"

She forced herself to sit down and behave. He wasn't a date, he was her bodyguard. And of the two of them she should be the better actress. But when he touched her, no matter how platonically, she wanted it to be real.

Wanted more. Wanted all of him.

She couldn't explain these outrageous reactions to him. They didn't know each other. In real life he might be just as much of a gold digger as her so many of her other dates had been.

"You promised me forty-eight hours," he said.

"N-not for this," she stuttered. "You're taking the part too seriously."

"Maybe I'm a method actor." He opened a bottle of water and handed it to her. "Nikki, when it comes to your safety, there's no such thing as taking it too seriously."

"Do you say that to all your clients?"

"I don't usually need to," he admitted. "Chicken salad or egg salad?" he asked.

He kept surprising her. "You're changing the topic?"

"I'm hungry," he admitted. "In your shoes, that interview alone would have done me in. And you put in hours ahead of that with rehearsal."

And the crisis he didn't mention. She focused on the food, once again impressed by the variety of options he'd ordered. Every bite was delicious.

"Is it rude of me to point out that none of this fare is typically available in the market?" she asked, spreading another bite of chicken salad on a crisp cracker.

"Curious?"

She couldn't turn it off. "You have this strange ability to just get what you want."

He laughed, the deep sultry sound sending her hormones into a tizzy. "All I did was make a call to the resort and they delivered. No special ops required."

He opened a small box, revealing stacks of powdered chocolate cookies about the size of a quarter. The rich scents had her mouthwatering, though she was sure she couldn't possibly take another bite of anything.

"Normally Ellington picnics include lemon cooler

cookies," Brett said. "Since it's the holidays we have mint meltaways."

She took one at his insistence and sighed with pleasure. The taste was amazing and the chocolate cookie melted away on her tongue. "What are lemon coolers?" she asked after she had another.

"How did you ever get away without them on your previous visits?" He tilted his head to the sky. "Think mint meltaway but lemon instead. I know that sounds dumb, but it's true. They are light as air and the perfect treat on hot summer days."

He made her want to come back and see a Carolina summer through his eyes. "The Ellington's have influence everywhere it seems."

"They're one of Charleston's founding families," he said. "They can trace the family back to one of the oldest land grants in history. And the family elders were smart about stewardship, community, and inheritance."

"It makes a difference to have a strong foundation," she said. "So many powerful families and couples in the entertainment industry have too much scandal and drama off-screen. I learned early how rare it was to have a stable family."

"Common sense and good support makes all the difference," he said. "I saw it growing up and during my service with the Navy."

The conversation moved toward other topics from his childhood to hers while she tried to ignore the occasional camera aimed at them. "Why did you join the Navy?"

"Service was expected to a point," he began. "It was never forced on me, but it felt right." He tapped his chest.

"And you got out and discovered you just can't stop protecting people?" She'd struck a nerve. She could see it in the tension popping in his jaw, but it was too late to take it back. He'd told her leaving the Navy hadn't been his choice. "Sorry. I didn't mean to pry."

"No worries." He smiled, but there was a sadness to it. "Being a bodyguard gives me a purpose and keeps me on my toes. "Now, I do mean to pry," he said with a wink, as they folded up the picnic blanket. Why did you stop making movies?"

"Well, part of it was age. There's a market for child actors and a market for adults. And there is a point when a woman doesn't look like either group."

"So it had nothing to do with the guy who got into your kitchen?"

Of course he would know about that. Who didn't? "I can't say that *wasn't* a factor," she admitted. "That whole mess was unnerving and the nonsense that followed wouldn't quit. People kept trying to break in. Others asked me to show them my moves. I'm not exactly proud of going into hiding, but I needed the space."

"About Haynes."

She steeled herself. "Yes?" Hadn't she put everything into the report?

"You never dated him?"

"Not once. He never even asked me out. All he's ever wanted is my name and money on one of his projects. He wants the shortcut to influence. He doesn't want to earn it. My lawyers and I have tried to straighten him out."

"I know." He slipped an arm around her before she got too wound up. "I know, honey."

Brett signaled for a rickshaw and helped her up into the seat. She didn't realize where they were going until he gave the direction to the driver. "Liberty Square?"

"It's not a bad walk, but we deserve the break," he replied. "I thought it was a good day for a harbor cruise."

She wasn't about to argue. Her body was tired. Not from effort as much as from tension of being on guard against Haynes's next move. It was nice to sit back and relax next to him. The conversation was strictly about the area, with the driver and Brett making sure she knew all the quirky details of the buildings and streets they passed. She wasn't even sure the driver recognized her and it was wonderful.

When they reached the pier, he surprised her again, ushering her onto a boat bound for Fort Sumter. The outing felt like a completely tourist move and she loved it. "I took this tour with Sadie on our last girl's weekend," she said.

"Huh. I didn't know they did wine and chocolate tastings on this ride," he teased.

"Only on the return trip." She bumped her shoulder to his. "Actresses can be smart too."

The heat in his eyes threatened to melt her like one of the cookies. "I noticed," he said.

They might as well have been the only two people in the world, his focus was that intense on her alone. In the past that kind of tunnel vision would have sent her running. From Brett it made her want to move closer, into his embrace, to really know the feel of that solid chest and those strong arms. He was so compelling. She was desperate to understand it, so that in the future when the time came, she would trust her instincts with men again.

Although she heard a few people whispering around them, no one tried to talk to her or ask for an autograph. And when they reached the fort, the focus shifted to the historical site, which pleased her immensely.

She could deal with polite, general curiosity. After all the media about the annual Nutcracker fundraiser, people were on the lookout for her around town.

"How you holding up?" he asked when the official tour ended and they were able to wander the grounds of the historical landmark for a bit before boarding the boat to go back.

"I'm good." And it felt good to say so. Brett had been polite and attentive, the perfect boyfriend. Not the least bit clingy or defensive. It was refreshing.

Plus, the outing had reinforced her faith in her intuition. She knew there were eyes on her, but there was no trace of malice. Not like when Haynes was close.

They were walking by the armory and she could see the situation the way the guide had described it. She could see it so clearly, those men carrying out their orders. Several movies had been done on the start of the Civil War, but she felt the stirring of another project in the back of her mind.

Passing by a family, she saw the flash of curiosity in the wide eyes of a mother and daughter when they recognized her.

Brett shifted, the move so natural it couldn't possibly offend anyone as he blocked their attempt to take her picture. He backed her into an alcove and kissed her.

It was better than last night and she had to work to remember this was an act. She was supposed to sell it, yet not get caught in an inappropriate scene. She broke the kiss, knowing she was grinning like a fool. "You're an expert," she said. She could believe he was so into her that he'd had to kiss her right then.

"I made a career out of evasion," he said. "The lessons stick."

"Good thing. I'm all wrong for a guy who likes being noticed."

He brushed his knuckle along her jaw and it took every ounce have her willpower not to dissolve into a puddle at his feet.

"From here, it sure feels like I'm with the right woman."

Just in case the kiss hadn't done it, those words sure did. Her heart slammed into her ribs, throwing itself at him, a man she'd known for less than a day. He was playing the part of new boyfriend too well. "We don't want to miss our ride," she said, lamely.

"Probably not."

On the ride back, the mother and daughter who'd wanted pictures at the fort approached her. This time, they asked politely for an autograph. She was happy to oblige and the moment turned into a good conversation all the way back to the pier.

"Would you like to walk or catch a ride?" he asked.

"Let's walk," she replied, surprising both of them. When he held her hand she felt like a normal couple on a holiday vacation. It was a delicious sensation and a day she would treasure forever, just for its simplicity.

"Thank you, Brett," she said as they neared the

parking garage. "I could get used to your style of protection."

BRETT HAD BEEN confident that his plan would put her at ease and make the job easier for the duration of their time together. But those kisses didn't feel pretend. What appeared to the world to be a date had gone very smoothly and he should be happy. Instead, it bothered him that basic courtesy and thoughtfulness seemed to be so out of the ordinary for her.

"Your schedule looks free for the evening," he said as they walked toward his parking space. "I was thinking it might be nice to drive through the Festival of Lights."

Sadie and Hank were talking about taking Emma tomorrow. Would you be willing to wait and make it a double date kind of thing?"

Was she using that phrase just in case someone was close? Or was she feeling this connection too? "Absolutely," he said. "There is nothing more fun than watching kids react to all those displays. She's the perfect age."

"Great." She pulled out her phone. "I'll let Sadie know."

He turned the corner and saw his car, grateful she was distracted. His windshield was smashed, a tire was flat, and he would bet the red mess splashed across the trunk and rear window was a blend of red paint and wine. Damn it.

Haynes knew how to make a point.

Brett blocked her view of the worst of the damage. "I forgot to return the picnic hamper," he said, turning her around.

He couldn't claim to know her well, but he suspected Nikki would feel guilty if she saw this. He'd never understood, why victims took on any guilt when a bad guy lashed out. No one could control someone else's actions. Trusting him to guide her, Nikki had yet to look up from her phone.

They were back on the street when she tucked her phone back into her purse. "Sadie says things went well today and they're excited about tomorrow."

"Glad to hear it. We should plan on barbecue beforehand. Are you up for another quick Market run?"

"Sure," she replied. "I thought I saw an author selling a Christmas book for kids. Emma might like that."

"Let's go." While she did that, he'd have time to notify Claudia and the police about the car. And call the resort for a lift back.

Knowing a car would take time to get out here at this time of day, he called the resort first. Then he returned the picnic basket to the Ellington Plantation booth. The author Nikki had noticed was just across the aisle, so he stood back and sent the news to Claudia by text.

Before Nikki paid for the book, his phone was blowing up with replies and instructions.

Police have been notified

Combing through security cameras in the area. Will compare w/images from area near theater

Police will take statements at resort. Bruce Ellington is expecting you

It was a relief when the car rolled up and he had to put the phone away so Nikki wouldn't see all the messages.

"WHEN ARE you going to tell me what happened?" Nikki asked as they slid into the back of the car. She'd played it cool while they were in public, but now she wanted answers. "Smart actress, remember?"

"I remember."

But he wasn't talking. "So what is this about? How exactly does your job involve a change up to a private car and driver?"

Here in the back seat of the town car, they didn't have to keep up the pretense, but he continued to touch her, to hold her hand on his thigh as if they'd been together for years. "My car was vandalized at some point today."

"What?" How had she missed this?

"Vandalized," he repeated. "You were texting Sadie."

"That's why we went back to the market."

He nodded. "Could be random."

He was way too casual about it all. "You do not think it's random," she accused.

With a sigh, he pushed his sunglasses up to his hair. "I don't. I got you out of there, per protocol. Then I called it in and let Claudia and the police take over. The police will want to visit with me. They agreed to meet with me at the resort."

"Haynes did this. All of it. Or he hired it done." She was fuming, but too well-trained to let the lid off her temper, not even in the back of a private car from an Ellington resort. "What else haven't you told me?"

"You're up to speed. One hundred percent," he said, looking miserable about it. He shifted, pulling out his phone with his free hand when it hummed.

"What now?"

"More of nothing," Brett replied. "Claudia says she can't get a good look at the face of the man in the garage, but the build matches up."

"Haynes is notoriously nondescript when he wants to be," she said.

"I assume that goes with a career in Hollywood."

"We are not all fake people," she snapped. She tried to tug her hand away, but he wouldn't let go.

"I know that," he soothed, his thumb stroking

over the inside of her wrist. "None of this feels fake to me."

He couldn't mean that, but he'd spoken too low for the driver to overhear. Her mind spun, wanting to believe him, but she'd be a fool to fall hard and fast for a man she'd just met, no matter how attentive, thoughtful and handsome.

"I haven't felt this alive since leaving the Navy," he said. "You, Nikki, are one of the warmest and most real people I've met. I will not allow this one selfish jerk to ruin your production or your life.

Her breath backed up in her lungs. She couldn't reply. Biting her lip to keep the emotions locked down, she turned to look out the window. How was it he always knew what to say?

"Nik. Look at me."

Relenting, she obliged. "I'm here for you," he said. "He won't run me off."

As he said it, she realized that was exactly what she feared most. That she'd be such a pain to protect that he'd give up, break his promises and leave her to cope with Haynes alone.

The car glided to a stop under the portico at the resort. "Let me do the heavy lifting here," he said. "All you have to do is shine."

He kissed her lightly on the lips and she knew she stepped out of the car looking soft and dreamy as any woman would after spending the day with her wonderful new boyfriend.

Bruce Ellington, head of resort security met them in the lobby. "A word in my office, Mr. Robinson? It won't take long," he promised Nikki with a smile.

"I'd prefer to join you," she said. "I think you'll need both of us." She wanted to hear it all firsthand. No filters. And she didn't want to be alone, not even here.

"Yes of course," Bruce replied.

Detective Marlow with the Charleston Police Department was waiting for them in Bruce's office. He was lean and tanned and spoke like a man who had all the time in the world to sort out this problem.

Nikki listened attentively to every detail as Brett relayed the previous night's attack along with the vandalism at the parking garage. Leaving her to confirm the details about the incident at the theater.

She had never taken it lightly when a member of her security team faced adversity. Yet these direct attacks on Brett felt different. More personal, as he'd said. Either Brett was a superb boyfriend actor or she was getting sappy. Either way, Haynes was escalating and she wanted Brett to be protected as well.

When the detective was satisfied, he thanked them and promised to be in touch. Bruce offered to have a meal delivered to her room, ensuring her complete privacy and she accepted.

"Dinner for two please," she said. "Do you have any lemon coolers?"

"I'm sure we do. Any wine?" Bruce asked.

"Not red," they replied in unison and a beat later, they were laughing.

With Bruce promising the meal would be delivered soon, Brett escorted her to her room.

"It's never gone down that way before," she said to Brett when they were finally alone.

"What do you mean?"

"In the past whenever I filed a report like that I've been grilled. Is this just a southern thing?" She unwound the bun at the back of her head and massaged her scalp. "Was it some effort to protect the little woman?"

"Hardly." A scowl marred his handsome face. "That's a big misconception about this part of the country. He took you seriously and asked smart questions, even though he had your statement about the theater incident."

"That's my point."

He stalked a little closer and she had to fight to hold her ground, but he didn't touch her. "You're used to being grilled about what you did to bring on each ugly encounter?"

"Yes," she whispered.

He swore. "We're not perfect around here, but this situation will not go down that way. I won't let Haynes get that kind of advantage on my turf."

She dared to step up, run her fingers over the buttons of his shirt. "I like your turf," she admitted.

She ruffled her fingers through his hair, wary of the goose egg he'd pointed out to the detective.

"You let me see your shoulder, but didn't mention this." Why wouldn't he kiss her?

"Getting jumped an hour into the job sort of defeats the whole bodyguard mystique. It's no big deal, I promise."

"Guess I'll take your word for it."

He bent his head, feathering kisses over her lips. Her pulse pounded in her ears, so that she didn't hear the first knock from room service.

"Hold that thought," he said, moving to answer the door.

More of that southern charm. She fluttered a hand over her heart, hoping she could handle it.

CHAPTER 6

THE NEXT NIGHT, after a grueling dress rehearsal at the theater, Nikki and Brett joined the Patterson's for a barbecue dinner before heading out to the Festival of Lights in Hank's rented SUV. Emma's delight over the displays was infectious and they were all smiling as they took part in various crafts, enjoyed a sing-along and worked up an appetite for s'mores.

This is how life would be with him. With a man *like* him, she amended quickly. Sadie had the same thing with Hank: absolute trust, abiding love, and protection when necessary. Maybe she should have accepted Sadie's offer for one of Hank's men to get involved and revamp her security earlier.

Of course if she'd done that, she wouldn't have met Brett and that would have been a tragedy.

"You've lost the Christmas spirit already?"

She blinked rapidly and gazed up into Brett's

smiling face. His dark hair was ruffled by the breeze and she suspected the chocolate smear on his chin was from the little boy he'd been helping build a s'more a few minutes ago. She had a ridiculous urge to lick his chin, shaking it off, she realized she had no clue what he'd said. "Pardon?"

He slipped his arm around her waist, strong and warm. If the music had been right, she would've flowed right into a swaying dance with him. But they were in a park, surrounded by people and children and cameras. And possibly Haynes. She stiffened at the thought.

"Easy, now. We're here to have fun." His eyes were full of mischief.

No one looking at him would think he was preoccupied with protecting her. And people accused her of being an excellent actor.

"You're flanked by two of the most capable men in town."

"So humble," she teased, playing her part. "Wouldn't that be the most capable 'in the world'?"

His carefree expression flinched just the tiniest bit. Only she was close enough to see. "Can't speak for Hank, but officially I don't see well enough to fire a gun for Uncle Sam, remember?"

The admission of any weakness surprised her. Whatever the trouble, it didn't seem to hamper him out here in the civilian world. "Sam's loss, my gain." She moved into him, swaying side to side as a perked up rendition of a Christmas classic played on the speakers.

He surprised her again, guiding her into the steps of a Carolina Shag to the swing of the music. Having learned the steps on a previous girl's weekend and taken enough dance classes in her early years, she kept up with him. "You are one revelation after another this evening," she said.

Giving her a spin and bringing her back in close, his grin was infectious. "I'm a Carolina boy through and through."

A few people noticed them and cheered, others joined them, including Sadie and Hank, who held Emma in his arm. Cameras flashed and she just didn't care. When the song ended and Brett brought their dance to a close with a grand flourish, applause erupted. This was a sweet and real moment, the kind of joy she'd relegated to people who weren't her.

"Maybe we should alter the afterparty and put in a dance floor," she said when they were on the way home, Emma nodding off in her car seat. Nikki was buckled into the center seat, Brett a warm and tempting presence at her back. He'd stretched his arm across the seat back, his fingertips tracing circles on her shoulder. He should know he didn't need to play the role in front of the Patterson's. Maybe, like her, he was falling for their act too.

Or maybe Christmas was going to her head.

"If I was in your cast, I'd rather just chill," Sadie

replied from the front passenger seat. "Then again, they are dancers. You'll have music going, right?"

"Right."

"So if they want to dance, they'll make a way. It'll be more fun if it's impromptu and no one feels obligated."

"Fair point." At least she thought it was. Brett's feathery touches were too distracting for her to be certain.

The rest of the drive back to the resort passed in a sparkling blur of lights. Though she kept up a quiet conversation, Nikki's mind was on how to get Brett to agree to a nightcap. In her room. The dancing had set her system on a slow simmer and she was more than ready to boil over.

BRETT NEVER SHOULD'VE DANCED with her. Now he couldn't stop touching her. She didn't seem to mind, a plus, but he was torturing himself. His thoughts weren't on the job. Not even close. His mind had locked onto the feel of her moving with him through the dance and extrapolated that to how they would move together privately. In a bed.

He left the car and deliberately scanned the surroundings before helping her out. Inside the lobby, she said goodnight to the Patterson's while he went to the front desk. He asked for any messages and checked his phone to be sure he hadn't missed a call.

She smiled, her deep blue eyes warm as she joined him. "Everything okay?"

"All clear," he replied. "Here at the resort and no news from Claudia either."

"That's good?"

"Only thing would be hearing Haynes was eaten by a gator," he said.

"Your Carolina Boy is showing again." She curled her fingers around his elbow.

"Is that a problem? I can reel him in."

She shook her head. "I like you just as you are, Brett."

"Thanks." Lame, but he didn't know the proper reply in this situation. "I like you too, Nikki."

The rest of the walk to her suite was made in a silence loaded with anticipation. And when they reached her door, she caught the panels of his jacket and pulled him inside the alcove with her. They weren't exactly on display, but they weren't completely hidden either.

As if she sensed his concern, she pressed to her toes and nipped at his bottom lip.

"Are we alone?"

"Aside from the security cameras, I think so."

He'd barely gotten the words out when she captured his mouth, her tongue stroking across his. He groaned, his body hard and ready from only that first hot lick of pleasure. He should be the professional and walk away. Let her go.

He stayed, spearing his hand into her hair and angling her for a deeper kiss.

This—kissing her, holding her—wasn't about playing a role and protecting her from Haynes or fans hoping for a selfie with one of the most famous women on the big screen. No, this was about two people and a crazy attraction that wouldn't quit.

The night had been so normal. They'd been a regular couple enjoying a holiday evening out with friends. Though he was the new addition to their circle, he shared an affinity with Hank, thanks to their shared history as Navy SEALs. And he liked Sadie and little Emma too.

But he was utterly lost to Nikki.

Her head fell back and he feasted on the soft silk of her throat.

"You should come in and check my room," she said, her voice like rough velvet.

"Smart." He should've thought of that perfect excuse.

She fumbled with her key card and he nudged her inside the minute the door opened. There, he took her in his arms, leaning back against the door and turning the deadbolt.

He could kiss her for hours, just like this, his hands cruising over her curves, his senses full of her. Smoke from the fire clung to her hair and her sweater. The sweetness of marshmallows and choco-late lingered on her lips and tongue. Under it all, was that fresh citrus with a kick of spice that was all Nikki.

"You smell like everything good about Christmas," he said, nuzzling her ear.

She trembled, her fingers gripping his scalp as she held him close. "Take me to bed, Brett. Stay the night."

He paused. A certain part of his anatomy twitched in eager expectation of what that invitation entailed. Afraid clarification would spoil the moment, he couldn't get this wrong. She was too damn impor-tant. "You want me to stay and keep watch while you sleep?"

Her laughter was a sexy ripple. "Only if that's a euphemism for as many orgasms as we can pack into the hours between now and my morning run with Sadie."

"Oh." Tracing the slope of her breast through the thick cotton weave, he stopped short of her peaked nipple. She arched, then grabbed his hand and put it right where she wanted it. Arching, into a caress she guided. He flicked that hard tip with his thumb and dipped his head for another kiss.

Her hips flexed into his. She was panting, clutching his shoulders. "Brett, please."

The need in her voice fired his blood. She was glorious and he was only human.

"No euphemisms. I want to be clear about this," he said.

She took his head in her hands, her gaze locked with his. "Stay because I need you," she said. "I need everything you make me feel. More." Her gaze fell to his mouth and she traced his lips with her thumb. "I need *you*, Brett. I need you to take everything I want to give. To you."

This was no pretense, no performance between them now. This was raw. Real. He let her shove his jacket off his shoulders, then he tugged her sweater over her head and tossed it to the floor. For a moment, he reveled in the stunning view of Nikki in only a sheer black bra and her favorite jeans.

The woman was glorious. He cupped her breasts and suckled her nipples through the fabric until she broke them apart to get his shirt off. He boosted her up and she wrapped her arms around his neck, her legs circling his hips. She giggled between kisses as he carried her to the big bed. Falling with her into the soft mattress, he filled his hands with her, tasted every inch of her bared flesh as it was revealed to him. Savoring each spot even as he craved what would come next.

Words failed him. She must have heard she was beautiful a million times from countless people who became a blur in her memory. He didn't want to be relegated to a cloud of fans this time. He wouldn't settle for offering up what the world had given her without any thought or knowledge of the amazing person inside the perfect package.

For tonight, he wanted to give her more. More than an orgasm or ten. He wanted her to feel a release, body and soul. A true release from the fear that haunted her day in and day out. This wasn't about how they'd met or the new-boyfriend trap they were setting for Haynes. Tonight was about the two of them alone, apart from the nonsense outside this room.

He set a slow pace, learning what made her arch and sigh, discovering where she was most sensitive. She loved the attention he lavished on her breasts and he reveled in the way her fingertips dug into his shoulders, holding him close. He slid a hand between her thighs, teasing her slick folds. She was as ready as he was. Her hips bucked as he lightly flicked that bundle of nerves.

She gasped his name while he suckled at her breast, stroking lightly over that sweet spot while he felt the first orgasm building. Her muscles quivered, her breath going quick and shallow, until on a low moan she arched up off the bed. Her skin was flushed, her eyes heavy as that first climax ebbed.

Conquerors didn't know this kind of victory.

"Brett," she reached for him.

He obliged in a kiss that seared his senses, while her hands petted his back. It was almost enough to make him want to hurry. Almost. Kissing a path down her body, he settled between her legs, holding her supple thighs still as he put his mouth to her most sensitive spot.

She reached to block him and he backed off, watching her face while he licked and kissed her fingers instead. "Show me what you want," he suggested, holding her gaze. "How you want it."

"I want you, inside me now."

He could tell it cost her. "In a minute."

"Brett."

"You're the one who mentioned multiple orgasms."

She laughed, a sexy breathless sound, and he kissed the inside of her updrawn knee. "Show me what you need."

Slowly, shyly, she moved her fingers over her flesh, pleasuring herself while he watched. It was the hottest fucking thing he'd ever seen. When she dipped a finger inside her channel, he glided one of his in as well. She groaned. He blew across her clit and she rocked her hips up close enough for him to lick her right there. Irresistible.

On a long, low 'yes', her fingers dug into his hair, holding him where she needed him while he took over, following the pattern she'd demonstrated with his tongue. She crested again in a gorgeous, shuddering explosion.

"Now, Brett, please. Please now."

God, yes. He grabbed the condom from his wallet

and rolled it over his aching erection. He'd never been so hard in his life. Braced over her, he meant to slow things down, but Nikki wasn't having that. She flexed her hips and used her legs to pull him deep. He met her demands, her channel gripping him in a tight heat that wouldn't quit until he was driving hard, thrust after thrust. Her body clenched around his shaft and this time when she climaxed, he was right there with her, riding a wave of indescribable pleasure.

As the aftershocks settled, he disposed of the condom and came back to the bed, holding her close and hoping like hell she wouldn't change her mind about him staying the night.

CHAPTER 7

THE NEXT MORNING, Sadie was waiting, splitting her attention between her family and her friend when Nikki came across the dunes.

"My, my. Someone looks rosy and relaxed this morning." Her grin was shameless. "I'm betting it is not just the sunshine that put that glow in your cheeks."

Nikki feigned innocence. "It's the Christmas spirit," she replied, somehow managing not to look back and see if Brett was watching her from the balcony.

"I'll buy that." Sadie peered back at the resort. "If your version of Santa Claus involves a former Navy SEAL who looks like sin in sunglasses and dances as smooth as the devil himself."

She would not fall for Sadie's tricks. Instead, Nikki gave her friend an exaggerated once-over from head to toe and then picked up the pace to an easy jog. "You should talk. After this trip I wouldn't be surprised if next Labor Day is actually a day of labor for you."

Sadie ran a hand lightly over her belly, a smile on her face. "That would be fine with us," she said. "Even better if you would hurry up and give Emma someone to play with on these trips."

Nikki couldn't deny a recent, if faint, yearning for motherhood. Maybe it was natural since she was on the verge of thirty. Just part of being female.

"I saw your face last night," Sadie said. "When Brett helped that little boy toast the marshmallow, you were the one melting."

There was no sense denying it. No sense in pretending she hadn't had the time of her life last night. At the festival and afterward in her room. There was also no sense in pretending it could be something more than it was. "He's a bodyguard. A pretend boyfriend. I told you that at the start so you wouldn't get stars in your eyes."

"Me?" Sadie snorted. "I'm looking at your face right now. That's where all the stars are. Why couldn't he be more, Nik? I mean, people have to meet and fall in love somehow."

"You know why."

"I know you've been burned," Sadie allowed. "And I understand better than most all the reasons you are afraid to trust. But living afraid isn't actually living."

She'd felt alive last night with Brett. Safe. Adored,

but in a clean, empowering way. The entire conversation cut a little too close to the bone. "I was talking about geography," she said.

"Don't you dare lie to me." Sadie gave her a small shove toward the water.

"Fine." Nikki regained her stride and confessed, "I was living plenty last night."

Sadie cackled so hard she lost her breath. Doubled over, she had to stop running until she recovered. Nikki jogged in place. "Good for you," Sadie said as they turned back. "Real sex during a pretend fling sounds like just the right recipe."

"For disaster."

"But what a way to go," Sadie said.

Maybe. Waking up beside Brett hadn't scared Nikki the way it should've done. She didn't feel crowded or judged or anything ugly. Only that strange contentment and peace. And that was knowing Haynes was out there. Not even the headlines that popped up on her phone, showing her dancing with Brett put her off.

Nikki appreciated that she could count on Sadie for perspective and much-needed humor. But trusting Brett with her body was different than trusting him with her heart. Wasn't it?

Had to be. Nothing else made sense. She couldn't possibly be falling in love with a man she'd just met. Not with her track record. Real sex, pretend fling. Nothing had felt false or pretend about last night.

Brett had all the right moves, in bed and out. The cynic in her wanted to argue it was just for show, a routine he could only apply on a temporary basis to get the job done. And she was his current job. The hopeless romantic in her still believed in the magic of Christmas, the season of miracles. That piece of her was more than halfway in love with Brett before she'd seen him naked.

It was *almost* enough to wish they wouldn't catch Haynes and Brett would feel obligated to stay with her. More time was what she needed. Time to figure out if all this happy tumult in her belly was the real deal.

FROM THE OCEAN-SIDE BALCONY, Brett kept an eye on Nikki for the whole run. He had walked her downstairs and once she was with Sadie, returned to his room to clean up and prep for the day, which included meeting back in her suite for breakfast. She didn't mention their forty-eight hour deal, and he wasn't about to bring it up and give her an excuse to ditch him. As far as he was concerned, employed or not, he was on duty until Haynes was under control.

Plus, he had a real date to plan. After last night, he was full of ideas. He just had to decide and set things in motion.

"Are you listening?" Claudia demanded.

"Yes." It wasn't a complete lie. "I'm multitasking."

"Prove you're good at it," Claudia said. "What did I just tell you?"

"You were talking about Haynes's track record. More victims beyond Nikki. You've found claims of harassment ranging from creepy peeping to getting grabby-hands on set."

"That's right." Claudia sighed. "You were listening."

"I always listen to my tech assistants." He waited for the burst of laughter to die down. "I know he wants her influence," Brett said. "But why Nikki? There are plenty of other women with means and power who are still in California."

"She hasn't told you?"

"No." He did his best to keep her mind off Haynes.

"Huh." Claudia sounded concerned. "I might have a theory on that, but I definitely have a location on him."

Everything inside Brett went still, a predator pausing, judging the killing blow. "I'm waiting." He took down the address on a piece of paper and then plugged it into an area map. The man was staying less than a mile away." Brett would work out something with Hank and Bruce to keep Nikki safe while he went to speak to Haynes. He didn't want Nicki anywhere near this guy.

"You can't just barge in there," Claudia reminded

him. "There are laws in South Carolina you must obey."

"Have you ever heard of the lawyers needing to bail me out of jail?" Although the Guardian Agency took separation of personnel to near extremes for security purposes, every so often Tyler would share a rumor about one of the bodyguards spending an hour or two in lockup. Minor infractions and misunderstandings, but no less stuck until Gamble and Swann sent someone to clear up the trouble.

"I'll handle it," he promised.

"Tactfully," she suggested.

"Of course." He checked the beach, making sure Sadie and Nikki were still fine, then scrolled to the newest email Claudia had forwarded with background on Haynes. He whistled low. "You've done some digging."

"More like turning over rocks," she said. "This guy is slime. Nikki never made him any outright promises. As far as I can tell, she never made him any vague promises either."

"And still he has it in his head she owes him. Convinced the general public too."

"Yup. I know you'll read all the details, but to sum it up, he felt cheated when a directing job went to her three years ago. His directing career has been in a tailspin ever since. I'm ninety-nine percent sure he's behind two different protests on her sets, though he claims that's random coincidence and no one can prove it. As you know, he's charmed many a Hollywood reporter along the way."

It confirmed his suspicions of how Haynes preferred to operate, from safely behind the scenes. Yet he was still fairly sure it had been Haynes himself who'd taken a direct swing at him that first night. "So we're agreed on that point," he said. "He knows how to hire people and twist perception. Nikki claims optics are everything."

"In this era she's right," Claudia confirmed. "Without hard evidence, or a direct attack caught on a camera somewhere, people will continue to see a rivalry, painting her as the untouchable diva bullying the underdog."

"What horseshit," he grumbled. "I'm hoping a new boyfriend will change the narrative."

"Just watch your back, Brett. He got too close too soon, for my liking. The fact that he followed her to Charleston feels more personal than his attempts to manipulate her in the past."

He tried to laugh off her concern, but he got distracted. Nikki was down on the beach, stretching with Sadie and her little girl. He wanted to get down there, but Hank and the other men on Bruce's team were close enough to prevent trouble.

"Does Nathan know you worry about other men?" Brett joked. Nathan and Claudia were the only two agency teammates he knew of who had met in person. Not only met but somehow managed to fall in love and get married. He wasn't sure how they managed a relationship in this line of work, but Claudia was as happy as he'd ever heard her on the other end of the phone.

"Hey, have you heard anything on Tyler?"

The silence was deafening, compounded by the hesitation. "That's the man I am really worried about," Claudia admitted, her voice low. "I'm told he's on a personal project, but no one gave me a timeline. If it's what I think it is, I'm afraid it will consume him."

He knew she wasn't complaining about any extra workload, Claudia was beyond capable. She was genuinely concerned for her counterpart, a young man she most likely had never met personally.

"He'll be fine." He didn't know what else to say. "I'm glad you've got my back on this one." He missed Tyler's irreverent voice in his ear, taking care of the details and guiding him through sticky terrain.

"If it comes up, you can tell Gamble and Swann that whatever Tyler needs, I'm happy to help. Once we catch Haynes." No chance in hell he was leaving Nikki alone to deal with the unpredictable jerk tormenting her.

"That means a lot," Claudia said. "Be sure you coordinate with your client about the headlines. I'm seeing more tabloid stuff pop up."

He groaned. "Bad?"

"More like adorable. I had no idea you had such great dance moves."

He rolled his eyes even though she couldn't see the reaction. "Want me to give Nathan lessons sometime?"

"His moves are just fine," Claudia said.

"And on that note," he said, "my client needs me."

He ended the call on her laughter. Down on the beach, Nikki didn't need him. She had her head close to Sadie's and the two were looking at a tablet of some sort. He did a quick internet search for news on Nikki and was immensely grateful for Claudia's warning.

Though he wouldn't change a single thing about last night, from the s'mores to the dancing to holding her all night long, anyone looking at these photos would see two people completely enamored with each other.

His feelings were on full display in these pictures, though he was supposed to be pretending. He wondered how much of the delight on her face was an act.

Damn. He was amazed Haynes hadn't made a scene already this morning.

And then his phone started ringing. If he had to guess, his normal date plans were about to be put on ice.

NIKKI KNOCKED on Brett's door, Hank and Bruce flanking her. Nerves jangling, she couldn't get the threat out of her head. Direct. Mean. Violence pulsed through her veins as she envisioned dishing out bodily harm to Haynes.

The only good news was that they were having this meeting in his room rather than hers, where there was still evidence that she'd had a very interesting night.

The door opened and she drank in the sight of him, dressed for another day downtown as her handsome shadow. Jeans and topsiders, a blue checked shirt with the sleeves rolled back. His hair damp from a shower. Her mind took a happier detour, thinking of Brett in the shower, hot water rolling over all those sexy muscles.

"What happened?" he asked, stepping back to let them in.

"Check it out." Hank handed over the phone. "It belongs to Sadie. She left it in the beach bag while they went running."

"It started ringing a few minutes after we got back," Nikki took up the story. "He was watching somehow," she said through gritted teeth. "Look at the text messages."

He did. Felt a pinch of fear between his shoulders as he scrolled through bomb threats at the theater along with pictures of Sadie and Brett, each with a promise of violence. "These are direct threats against the performance. He used a number registered to his own name."

"I have police on the way," Bruce said. "I've notified the security team at the theater as well."

"That's a good start. My assistant found where Haynes is staying. Let's get someone out there as well." He gave Bruce the information and the older man started making calls.

She waited, afraid of what he would say next.

His gaze landed on hers, all business, no hint at all that he remembered what she looked like naked. "It's opening night," he said.

"It is."

"You want to cancel?"

She thought of the impact to the company and the charities that were counting on a boost from tonight's ticket sales. Thought of the risk to the historic theater itself. "Is it safe to go on?"

"It can be." He leaned back against the edge of the desk. She saw files scattered behind him. This was the professional bodyguard, the former SEAL, an expert at battle strategy. "Hank and I can go through the building."

Hank nodded his agreement.

"There is nothing in his file that suggests he would know the first thing about explosives. Of all these threats, I think that's bogus." He read the texts again, took the time to review the pictures.

"Doesn't mean he won't cause trouble," Hank said.

"Right. But we can add officers, call in support from an extra company, and make sure everyone knows his face."

"But there's still a risk."

"Your call," Brett said. He glanced past her to Bruce. "It's also possible that we'll have him wrapped up before the doors open."

"Police are headed to the property," Bruce said. "I'll go over as well, in case there's anything from the resort in his possession."

"Keep us posted," Brett said as he walked out.

"Will do."

Again Brett's pale blue gaze met hers. "You and Sadie will stay here with Emma."

"In the room," Hank clarified. "Bruce has offered to post security on the floor and at the door."

She shook her head. "I want to go with you," she said to Brett. "Haynes came here because of me," she added in a rush. She could see he was about to refuse her request.

Brett and Hank exchanged a long glance but no words. It must have been a military thing. She waited for the verdict.

He relented and she nearly flew into his arms, forgetting Hank was right there. He understood the burden she carried. No, she wasn't responsible for the actions of Gus Haynes, but she was inextricably tied to the jerk.

"Thanks," she managed. "I'll be ready in fifteen

minutes." She was out the door before either man could come up with another reason for her to stay behind.

The hours that followed were a dreadful waiting game, watching Brett, Hank, and a police officer and his K9 partner trained in explosives search the theater. Finally they gave the all clear.

As she was changing clothes for the opening performance, Brett informed her that Bruce and the police had scoured Haynes's room. The man was in the wind, but they found the uniform shirt he stole from the Ellington resort as well as his plans to kidnap her from the theater amid the chaos of a bomb threat evacuation.

"So we're clear?" she asked, putting on her earrings.

"Clear as we can be considering Haynes is still loose," he replied cautiously. "I'll be with you every step of the way."

She smiled, handing him her necklace and turning so he could secure the clasp. His fingers brushed her bare skin, giving her a thrill that would keep her blood humming all night.

"Then everything will be just fine."

He studied her for a long moment and she silently wished for his kiss.

At last he brushed his lips over hers, enough to tantalize, not nearly enough to satisfy. "You're going to steal the show."

"I won't even be on stage."

"*Mmm.* That's a real shame."

This time when he kissed her, she had to check her lipstick when it was over. "You'll stay with me again tonight?"

"Can't think of anywhere I'd rather be."

He meant it. Her heart positively soared. His genuine interest in *her*—not what she might do for him—was as wonderful as the passionate kisses he lavished on her.

CHAPTER 8

NIKKI TOOK A DEEP BREATH, clutching Brett's hand in both of hers. Tears of joy blurred her vision for just a moment. The initial forty-eight hours had passed without firing Brett or catching Haynes. She'd lost the wager, but the demands of the performances and the continuing search for threats hadn't left much time for that normal date she owed him.

But now it was over and it felt as if a weight had lifted from her shoulders. Haynes hadn't interfered with the sold-out shows. She was safe, her cast was safe, and the audience was safe. Now, she could relax.

The applause and shouts of bravo swelled as the ensemble took another bow. Flowers hit the stage in a colorful avalanche to the utter delight of the younger performers. They'd earned it. She was content to celebrate the successful run from the wings, Brett within arm's reach. The spotlight was nice, but on this occasion she was little more than a figurehead for fundraising purposes.

"You have to go out there," he murmured, his breath warm against her ear.

A delicious tremor rippled down her spine. She was hoping for a private celebration, just the two of them, after the party. For right now, she turned into his arms, her full skirt brushing across his slacks as she kissed him on the lips.

"Thank you, hunky new boyfriend."

"My pleasure, sexy new girlfriend."

Of course the charade would be over soon. He seemed to think they were closing in on Haynes after finally locating his room in a hotel not far from the resort. Close enough to come in to the bar and send her that awful note. Close enough to attack Brett that very first night, vandalize his car, and cause havoc during the final rehearsal.

But thanks to Brett, his most disturbing threats had been rendered useless and his attempts to harass her, foiled. Brett had done that. Brett's leadership and high standards had restored her faith in people. No one had betrayed her location or given the media anything to use against her. It was a Christmas wish come true. One of them anyway.

With another quick glance to her personal hero, she shook out her skirt and stepped onto the stage when her name was announced, confident Haynes was not in the theater. She didn't have any logical reason to believe it, but she hoped he'd left town. Given up.

Still, she didn't tempt fate by lingering in the spotlight. Taking the mic just long enough to thank the crowd, the city, and praise the theater community as a whole for their superb work and performance.

"On behalf of all of us," she said wrapping up her short speech, "it's my pleasure to wish each of you a Merry Christmas and all the best for the New Year."

She took one more bow, the cast surrounding her, and then the curtain came down. This time when the applause faded, a softer rumble replaced it as the audience moved to the exits. The dancers and crew made quick work of changing clothes for the private afterparty at a nearby restaurant.

A week ago she would've worried over making the walk from the theater, even with friends around her. Tonight, she linked her arm in Brett's and enjoyed the boundless happy energy swirling through the beautiful night. "Have I mentioned how sexy you are in formalwear?"

"You have." He grinned at her. "Not as sexy as you," he said, pretending to leer down her dress."

She laughed. "December in Charleston is better than I expected."

"It sparkles more with you in it."

The man could make her heart flutter at will. "You're too kind," she said cozying up to him. She was going to miss him when she went back to California.

"Really, I'm not."

The low rumble of his voice was like an open flame warming her all over. She was about to suggest they only stay for one drink and then take it back to the resort when they reached the party. She'd booked the entire restaurant for a few late hours, paying a steep price for full staff on the holiday evening. She didn't regret a penny of the expense, seeing everyone smiling and bubbling over.

"This is why you do it," Brett said quietly. "You're practically glowing just watching them all have fun."

"They deserve it. They've worked so hard." It didn't surprise her that he'd figured her out. He had excellent observation skills. "I need to mingle a bit. You don't have to—"

"But I do." He raised his water glass and gently tapped it to her champagne flute. "Lead the way."

At her side he was a gracious companion, able to hold his own no matter where the conversation drifted. In the restaurant's back garden, sparkling with white string lights and colorful rosemary topiaries, she got a chill. Without a word, Brett removed his tuxedo jacket and draped it around her shoulders. She tipped up her face, pleased when he pulled her close for a moment, touching his nose to hers.

A camera flashed and she tensed up until she realized it was Sadie.

"It's one you'll want to keep," Sadie said.

Nikki wasn't so sure. She wouldn't forget a moment of her Charleston holiday with her sexy fake boyfriend. A picture might just make it harder to move on when they inevitably parted ways.

She watched Brett chatting with Hank while Sadie filled her in on the schedule for tomorrow. Santa would bring Emma's presents to the hotel. "We'd like to help you celebrate your birthday in the evening."

"I'd—" A sudden pressure at her side cut her off.

"Say good night, Nikki."

Haynes. Oh, God. Ice pulsed through her heart. Why wouldn't he leave her alone? How had he gotten in? The afterparty location was hardly a secret, but they had people watching for him.

She opened her mouth to scream, but he grabbed her by the throat while he fired the gun into the air. Hank and Brett were moving in before the sound faded. Hank tucked Sadie behind him and backed away. Brett kept coming, halting only when Haynes pressed the hot barrel of the gun into her side.

He held his hands out wide. "Let her go."

"No."

"There's no way out," Brett said, taking another step closer. "Plus you fired the gun. This is Charleston, cops will blanket this place within minutes."

He was talking to Haynes, but Brett's eyes were on her. There was a message in his gaze, some signal he wanted her to figure out. Her heart was pounding too hard, she could barely hear him, much less figure out his silent code.

"I'll be fine," Haynes snarled. He shoved the gun hard into her ribs. "I have the golden goose. Finally." His arm banded across her chest. "You and I will be Hollywood's next power couple. I have your part all written out."

"Never." He was crazy. There was no possible leverage he could use to make her agree to his plan. Just the gun and he couldn't hold that forever.

Brett took another long stride forward. "Take me."

"Back off!" Haynes aimed the gun at Brett.

Brett didn't flinch. "Come on. Now's your chance to shove me out of her life."

"No," she breathed.

"Me. Now." Brett tapped his chest. "Or I won't ever stop hunting you."

"No!" she cried, stronger. She'd never forgive herself if Haynes hurt Brett.

Haynes yanked her back, the gun biting into her side once more. As he dragged her away, her heel caught in a seam between pavers. She let herself fall back, letting her weight land against Haynes on her way to the ground.

Brett lunged for him and they crashed through the boxwood hedge that bordered the patio garden. She saw flashes as the men wrestled, only recognizing Brett because of his stark white shirt. Haynes had been dressed all in black.

He'd thought of everything, the bastard.

"He's running," Brett shouted. "To the cemetery."

Hank pulled out his phone and hit the flashlight app. The men and the light disappeared into the darkness, voices raised as they shouted directions to each other and the officers on site as they gave chase.

At the first gunshot, Nikki rushed toward the darkness beyond the party. Sadie caught her, holding her back. "Brett!" She smothered the cry behind her hands. The masculine scent of him surrounded her, warm and alive, but it was only his jacket. She wanted the man.

"You can't go out there," Sadie said. "Let them work."

Her friend was right. Nikki didn't have to like it, but she'd be a fool to rush into the chaos. All they could do was wait and pretend it would all be okay.

She was damned tired of pretending.

"If anything happens to him…." She'd claw the eyes right out of Haynes's head. "To either of them."

"They're the toughest thing this side of active duty," Sadie reminded her. "Haynes doesn't have a chance."

No, but he had a gun.

There was more shouting, sirens as more police arrived. She could only be grateful that the church wasn't holding a midnight service. The remaining guests gathered around, lending moral support.

Two more gunshots were heard, too close for comfort. Nikki prayed, gripping tightly to Sadie. But the reactions of the people flanking her weren't enough to block out the call for an ambulance.

"Who is it?" she said, rushing the officer nearest her. "Who was hit?"

Hank jogged out of the darkness before the officer could reply. "They're both down," he said. "We'll meet them at the hospital."

She shoved Hank aside and ran toward the cluster of lights to see for herself. He'd put himself in the line of fire for her. She couldn't leave him. He mattered and she was done pretending otherwise.

BRETT WALKED out of the exam room, expecting police to be waiting. Hoping to see Bruce Ellington or even Hank. He didn't know what to do when Nikki rushed toward him. He'd only seen her for a moment before they loaded him into the ambulance. He didn't even know if she heard him say it wasn't bad. Hadn't had time to ask if he'd hurt her.

Wrapped up in his tuxedo jacket, the glitter of her Christmas red skirt was a stark contrast. She looked small and vulnerable and he wanted to gather her close and never let go. But she was staring at him, arms folded across her midsection, and her defenses were up.

"Are you hurt?" he asked.

"What did they say?"

His question bumped into hers and they watched each other for a long moment. After being so easy with her for the past few days, so confident in reading her, now he had no idea what she was thinking or what she needed from him.

She moved first, reaching for him and then pulling back as if she was afraid her touch might hurt him. Not being touched hurt far more. "I'm fine," he said. "I told you it wasn't bad."

"He shot you," she said. "You were bleeding."

"Would you believe it was chocolate syrup?"

She rushed close and thumped her fist lightly on his chest. "Stop teasing me. What did they say?"

He wrapped her into a gentle hug, thankful for the contact. Then he lifted the hem of his stained tuxedo shirt, revealing the edge of the bandage covering the shallow wound. "The bullet grazed me. It's not much worse than a scrape." No thanks to Haynes. The man had done his best to put that bullet in his gut while talking trash about what he'd do with Nikki.

Brett clenched his teeth. They'd won. Haynes wouldn't bother her ever again. Brett catalogued every detail of her gorgeous face. The color was back in her cheeks, a relief after the pale and panic of an hour ago. "I'm fine," he repeated. "It's over and done."

"He's...he's dead?"

If only. "Last I heard, he's expected to live." Not for lack of trying, but Brett wasn't about to tell her the gory details.

She scowled.

"My agency has already forwarded everything you gave us on him to the Charleston police. That along with what Claudia dug up and what the police found in his hotel room will keep him behind bars for a long time." A dreadful thought occurred to him. "You are pressing charges? Adding those complaints to mine?"

"Yes," she said immediately.

"Good." He would've been furious if she'd balked at taking that step this time.

"It's really over," she whispered. "I'm not sure what to do now."

"Whatever you want." He was a fool to think he might rank on that list. In truth, he didn't know what to do next either. She didn't need a protective boyfriend at her beck and call anymore. But man, he'd be willing.

"Sadie and Hank are waiting," he said, spotting the couple near the waiting area. "They'll take you back to the resort.

"Me?" Her beautiful eyes clouded with confusion. "What about you?"

Brett tilted his head toward the police officers and Bruce, the head of resort security, waiting for him at the opposite end of the hallway. "I need to go," Brett said.

He wanted to beg her to let him stay close, wanted her to invite him back to her room when he was done with the police.

"There will be questions and…" And none of that mattered. Not really. He had plenty of witnesses to back up his side of the story, including the officers on the scene. "It's Christmas Eve. The more help I give them the sooner they can wrap this up and get home to their families."

"Right. I understand." She pressed up on her toes and kissed him. On the cheek. She might as well have sent him a break-up text. "Thank you," she whispered.

She stepped back and shrugged out of his jacket, handing it over. He didn't want the jacket, he wanted her, but she walked away, toward Hank and Sadie. Her friends. Her world, so far removed from his. Hank lifted his chin, silent acknowledgement that they'd keep an eye on her and get her back to the resort.

And after that? Who would make sure she celebrated her birthday properly? It should be him. Except they'd never claimed there would be anything after Haynes was contained. They were a temporary deal. Her project in South Carolina was done, to great acclaim despite the dustup at the afterparty.

He'd never felt so lousy after a job well-done. Well, he'd never fallen in love with his client either.

The awareness shocked him, left him breathless. Love. That's what it was. Pure and simple and thoroughly impossible. They were miles apart, separated by more than geography. She had more money and resources than she could ever use up. She could dictate terms on any career choices or personal endeavors that struck her fancy. All he could bring to the table was himself, except she didn't need his protection anymore.

He dared to look back, one final glimpse of the woman he wanted more than his next breath. To his surprise, he caught her looking at him.

Hope flickered, a flash of lighting in the dark cloud of despair hovering over his heart, and a new idea took root in the back of his mind.

Technically, she still owed him a date.

CHAPTER 9

JUST A FEW HOURS LATER, Nikki's birthday dawned bright and clear. She was free. Haynes was in custody, and he'd be in prison as soon as the hospital released him. He'd never be a problem again with so many witnesses to his brash party-wrecking attack.

She should be happy. Relieved. Joyful that for the first time the situation couldn't be turned around, couldn't be explained away as Nikki Weston being too selfish and full of herself.

That was all thanks to Brett.

She owed him everything and she might never see him again.

Glancing toward the bed, her body heated even as tears stung her eyes that she was alone.

Still.

Always.

Christmas wishes were fun, but they were merely

as fantastical as the classic production she'd just delivered to a packed house and thrilled audiences.

Wrapping herself in a hotel robe, she moved toward the balcony, hesitating to step outside into the cool ocean breeze and the brightening day. He had been with her the last time she'd done so. Her bravery boost, strong and warm at her back. Today, she didn't need protection but she desperately wanted his presence.

On the table beside the bed, her phone chimed with an incoming message. She hurried over, hoping it was him.

It wasn't. It was a happy birthday message from Sadie.

Nikki replied with heartfelt thanks, as she did every year, but this was the first time she didn't feel it.

"Enough." She spoke aloud, snapping herself out of her funk. It was her birthday and she'd made a plan weeks ago for how she wanted to greet thirty. Today would be better because she was free to enjoy every moment, no wondering or worrying about when Haynes would pop up and try to ruin it.

It was too cold for the birthday bikini she'd brought along, so she pulled on her favorite jeans and a cotton sweater. Bundling her hair into a messy bun, she found her flip flops and headed downstairs. At the coffee bar set up just outside the resort restaurant, she filled a to-go cup with the breakfast blend, adding an extra splash of cream. She didn't care just now who might snap a picture and post criticism online.

Coffee in hand, she walked toward the beach. Every step reminding her of Brett. The boardwalk where he'd first kissed her. It had been for show, but the chemistry, the sparks had been real. Sliding out of her shoes, she reached for him for balance, but he wasn't there.

This melancholy had to stop. It was a fling, the best of her life. He'd done his job, on multiple levels. It was up to her to make the most of that gift.

He'd demonstrated the type of man she deserved and set a new standard for her in the process. Integrity and kindness. Strength and humor. Passion and laughter. Sincerity above all else. It was a standard she would not relinquish, if it meant she was alone for the rest of her life.

That was the real gift, she thought as she strolled along the beach, just out of reach of the incoming tide, the sun warm on her shoulders and back.

Merry Christmas, happy birthday, and hallelujah! Nikki was done settling for a half-life. Sadie would be thrilled. Her parents would be delighted. Her agent would have a field day securing scripts for her to work on. She was ready to be in front of a camera again.

She sat down in the sand to watch the waves and drink her deliciously creamy coffee and think about what she wanted to bring about in the upcoming year. But her mind wouldn't stick with project ideas, only him.

Brett.

Closing her eyes, she listened to the rolling ocean, so different from the coast where she'd grown up. But it was all part of the same world. She wanted Brett to be part of her world. Or maybe she really wanted to become part of his.

Here, in the quiet vibrance of southern hospitality, with the gracious drawl, the sweet tea, and the big open-hearted acceptance.

No maybe about it, with or without Brett, she wanted to spend more time right here. Would he be interested? She reached for her phone and discovered she'd left it behind in her room. Oh, well. Probably better to give herself some time to find the right words. Right or wrong, one of Brett's best features was that he'd listen and give her an honest response.

Her coffee finished, her plan in mind, she popped up and hurried back to the resort to line up a few things. It was a holiday, she might have to wait until tomorrow when stores reopened.

Distracted, she didn't notice the activity on the beach until she was almost to the boardwalk that led back to the resort. A team of resort employees was feverishly setting up chairs and umbrellas and she nearly plowed into a young man carrying a bucket filled with champagne nestled in ice.

"Excuse me," she said, backing up to let him pass.

He gawked at her, his gaze darting to someone behind her. It was enough to have her bracing for trouble.

Not trouble. Brett.

Her entire body relaxed and his smile warmed her straight through. "Happy birthday."

"Thank you." He held out a hand and she bypassed it, going for a hug instead. When his arms came around her, she delighted in her bold decision. "I'm happy to see you," she said, drawing him away from whatever was going on behind them. He looked good and there was a hint of a smile on his lips. "Are you feeling all right?"

"Almost perfect." He stopped short. "You're going the wrong way, Nikki."

"What do you mean?" She'd just been thinking about moving in the right direction, for the first time in ages, stepping out in confidence rather than fear.

The staff had added several low tables to the setup and she wondered who had decided to overwork such a great crew on a holiday. She hoped they were being compensated.

"Your birthday party, is this way." Still holding her hand, he checked his watch. "Officially starting in ten minutes."

She could only stare at him, completely baffled by what she was hearing.

"One thing first." He gave her a little tug and as

she bumped into his chest, he caught her lips with his. He took his time with the kiss, letting it build slowly. The sweet tenderness overwhelmed her.

When he lifted his head, her heart pounded at the emotions swimming in his gaze. Could he possibly be feeling the same things she did? "I'm in love with you." She blurted it out, zero grace or poetry.

His eyes went wide and she felt a moment's fear. Either way, she'd get an honest reply. An honest rejection was better than anything fake. Although she couldn't help it that her heart wanted to hear one specific answer.

"Nikki." He rested his forehead to hers for just a moment. "You were supposed to be bowled over by the champagne. Impressed by my sneak attack and creative solutions."

"I already know what a creative problem solver you are." She drew him close for another kiss, hope pulsing through her veins.

"You were supposed to be impressed," he said again, giving her hands a squeeze. "And riding a happy sugar high when I asked you to stick with me."

"Stick with you?" Not quite the declaration of love she'd been hoping to hear.

"I'm rattled," he admitted, an adorable frown puckering his dark eyebrows. He took a deep breath. "I was going to ask you for more time. Together. On your coast or mine. Time to prove to you how good we are together, without pesky stalkers in the mix."

Her heart soared. "You don't ever have to prove anything to me." She knew they were good together. "But you live here."

"I've lived all over. Worked all over." He hooked her arm through his and walked her closer to the water's edge away from the party preparation. "So I know that wherever you are is home for me. I'm in love with you too, Nikki. Crazy as it sounds."

"It's the sanest thing I've heard in my life," she assured him. "I should've said it sooner."

"Sooner might have been before we met," he joked. "You're sure this isn't moving too fast for you?"

She wrapped her arms around his lean waist. "With the only man I've trusted beyond my dad and Hank? Not too fast at all." She kissed him again. She might be ready to stop in a decade or so. "I love you, Brett."

"I love you, too." He stroked her cheek. "There's a champagne breakfast and a cake with your name on it."

"Seriously?" Birthday cake for breakfast sounded divine. Delighted, she peered around his shoulder, as Sadie and Hank trailed their daughter across the sand to the party area. "Friends too, I see."

"Always."

She couldn't think of a more perfect birthday celebration. "Thank you," she said. She'd been preparing all month to take care of herself, again. Brett had given her so much more, become so much more in her life. "This is the best day of my life," she said. "Because of you."

"That's only fair," he said as they walked over to join the others. "Since every day with you is better for me than the day before."

This man. He kept surprising her in the happiest ways. She rested her head on his shoulder. "Want to see how long we can keep that going?" she asked.

"Oh, yeah." He pressed a kiss to her hair.

"Can we start that here? I love the Lowcountry almost as much as I love you."

"You've got yourself a deal," he said.

A waiter filled glasses with champagne and everyone sang happy birthday and here, surrounded by friendly faces and pure happiness stretching as far as the horizon, Nikki was ready to embrace the first day of a bright, beautiful, full life ahead of her.

The End

For full details on all of Regan's books visit ReganBlack.com and enjoy excerpts from each of her adrenaline-fueled novels.

Black Ice, Book 4 in Stormwatch, a multi-author series

what she knew, Book 4 in Breakdown, a multi-author series

Escape Club Heroes, Harlequin Romantic Suspense

The Riley Code, Harlequin Romantic Suspense

Colton Family Saga, Harlequin Romantic Suspense

Knight Traveler Series

The Matchmaker Series

ABOUT REGAN BLACK

Regan Black, a USA Today and internationally best-selling author, writes award-winning, action-packed romances featuring kick-butt heroines and the sexy heroes who fall in love with them. Raised in the Midwest and California, she and her husband share their empty nest with two adorably arrogant cats in the South Carolina Lowcountry where the rich blend of legend, romance, and history fuels her imagination.

For early access to new book releases, exclusive prizes, and much more, subscribe to the monthly newsletter at ReganBlack.com/perks.

Keep up with Regan online:
www.ReganBlack.com
Facebook
Twitter
Instagram

Or follow Regan at:
BookBub
Amazon

facebook.com/ReganBlack.fans

twitter.com/ReganBlack

instagram.com/reganblackauthor

BROTHERHOOD PROTECTORS

ORIGINAL SERIES BY ELLE JAMES

Brotherhood Protectors Series

Montana SEAL (#1)

Bride Protector SEAL (#2)

Montana D-Force (#3)

Cowboy D-Force (#4)

Montana Ranger (#5)

Montana Dog Soldier (#6)

Montana SEAL Daddy (#7)

Montana Ranger's Wedding Vow (#8)

Montana SEAL Undercover Daddy (#9)

Cape Cod SEAL Rescue (#10)

Montana SEAL Friendly Fire (#11)

Montana SEAL's Mail-Order Bride (#12)

SEAL Justice (#13)

Ranger Creed (#14)

Delta Force Strong (#15)

Montana Rescue (Sleeper SEAL)

Hot SEAL Salty Dog (SEALs in Paradise)

Hot SEAL Hawaiian Nights (SEALs in Paradise)

ABOUT ELLE JAMES

ELLE JAMES also writing as MYLA JACKSON is a *New York Times* and *USA Today* Bestselling author of books including cowboys, intrigues and paranormal adventures that keep her readers on the edges of their seats. With over eighty works in a variety of sub-genres and lengths she has published with Harlequin, Samhain, Ellora's Cave, Kensington, Cleis Press, and Avon. When she's not at her computer, she's traveling, snow skiing, boating, or riding her ATV, dreaming up new stories. Learn more about Elle James at www.ellejames.com

Website | Facebook | Twitter | GoodReads | Newsletter | BookBub | Amazon

Follow Elle!
www.ellejames.com
ellejames@ellejames.com

facebook.com/ellejamesauthor
twitter.com/ElleJamesAuthor

9 781626 952966